Murderers can't lie to God

Las Vegas murder stories
Book 1

M. Makuta

Published by Las Vegas Home Field Advantage, 2021

To Tunio

M. MAKUTA

Death must have been instantaneous. The forensics would figure out the details, but any of the three bullet wounds could have been fatal.

The body of a man lay in the center of an empty room. The blood from the wounds stained the off-white carpet. They would have to replace it now, even though the carpet smelled brand new. The smell of fresh paint was another sign that this remodel was complete and the house was ready for the market. It wouldn't bring top dollar now, not with a murder in it. Nobody wants to buy a house like that. "Too bad," thought Lieutenant Kiedron, because the house was very nicely done. The open concept kitchen plus the living room was airy and bright. The patio door opened to a comfortable yard with a sparkling pool and a hot tub. Tall palm trees framed the view of the famous Las Vegas strip. It looked good now. It would look gorgeous at night.

Other than the body, a small handgun next to it, and an unused sandwich bag next to the gun, the room was empty. There was no furniture, no pictures on walls, nothing at all to add personality to the interior.

The freshly renovated kitchen was also empty except for a cell phone on the counter next to the sink --- the victim's, most likely.

Lieutenant Stan Kiedron of the Las Vegas Metropolitan Police Department eyed the scene, carefully taking in the details. The blood spatter, the position of the body, the placement of the gun, all this made sense. The sandwich bag? That was unusual. It was not only empty, it looked like it had never been used. Why was it here?

The room was crawling with people. The crime scene investigator was taking pictures from every angle imaginable. Forensics techs were sweeping the house for fingerprints and other clues.

"David Chepstow," detective Jaq Ashfield identified the body from the driver's license she fished out of the victim's wallet, which she had just pulled from his pocket and handed to Kiedron.

"You shouldn't have," he gave her a stern look. "The body belongs to the ME," he explained in response to her confused expression. The medical examiner, or the ME, was the only one that was allowed to touch a dead body at a crime scene. At least that was the protocol, although sometimes it didn't work out this way. Kiedron shrugged. What's done is done.

"The address is Dragon Ridge, MacDonald Ranch," he read. "One of the most expensive parts of town."

"Figures," Jaq nodded. "Look at his watch."

MURDERERS CAN'T LIE TO GOD

Kiedron looked. He expected something flashy, a Rolex maybe. Instead, the watch was understated, and the brand unknown to him. "IWC. What about it?" he asked, puzzled.

"Swiss. International Watch Company. You could buy a nice car for what this one costs," Jaq explained.

This wasn't the first time that Kiedron was quietly thanking his lucky stars for taking a chance on hiring this rookie young detective. The quirky things she knew often saved a ton of research time.

"How do you know this?" he asked. She smiled.

People in the department didn't know what to make of Jaq. She joined just a few weeks ago, and it was hard to get to know her. She didn't go out to drink with the guys, never sat down with them to pig out on donuts and gossip. She was completely focused on her work and socialized with no-one.

Although people didn't talk much to her, they talked about her plenty, mostly about how she was weird. She never wore makeup, her mousy brown hair was severely pulled back and tied mercilessly at her nape into the tightest bun from which no hair dared to escape. Her nondescript clothes were always several sizes too big. She could be skinny, or fat, and nobody could tell. Someone tried calling her Jackie and got an earful. There was nothing soft or feminine about her. Some people in the department started wondering if she was gay. But then, she showed no interest in women either. She focused on her work and didn't care one bit about being liked.

"When do you think he died?" Jaq asked Kiedron.

He frowned. Estimating the time of death wasn't an exact science. "I'd guess yesterday afternoon or evening. The ME should tell us more precisely. Speaking of the devil..."

Dr. Stopa ran into the room and squatted by the body. She was a tough little woman of undetermined age, skinny and muscular, with very short black hair and blue eyes that were set too close together. She examined the body carefully and pointed to the victim's jacket.

"There is a hair on his chest. You might as well collect it now."

An investigator placed a tag on the victim's chest next to the hair, took a picture, and then carefully removed the hair with a pair of tweezers. It was long and blond, definitely not the victim's. He placed the hair in a paper bag.

Investigators use both paper and plastic bags for storing evidence. The protocol specifies that paper must be used for any biological evidence where possible. This is because closed plastic bags create an environment for bacteria to grow, and this could contaminate the evidence. In the case of a hair, it probably wouldn't matter, but the protocol is protocol.

Detective Bill Stockton came in from the garage through the inside door. He was another young detective that Kiedron took under his wing, hiring him just a couple of months before Jaq. He was tall and chubby. With very short blond hair, blue childlike eyes, and rosy complexion, he looked innocent and much younger than his years. He used his looks to make people feel at ease, which was a great plus in interrogations.

"Lieutenant, there is a car in the garage," he announced. "The glove compartment is open."

Kiedron nodded and stepped into the garage. That's one more thing the forensics team needed to check. The more data the better, although most likely the car belonged to the victim, because how else did he get here? An open glove compartment was another unusual thing to check out, just like the empty sandwich bag on the floor. It didn't make sense now, it should later. Kiedron didn't like loose ends. After the crime was solved, every detail should make sense.

Kiedron looked carefully at the car, a white Tesla. The inside still smelled brand new. A member of the forensics team was working on the car, so Kiedron decided to get out of the way. He walked back into the house and took another look around.

"Who found the body?" Kiedron asked Stockton.

"The cleaning lady. She's waiting outside."

"Anybody else I need to talk to outside?"

"No sir," said Stockton. "We have everybody's info so we can contact them if we need to, but nobody had anything helpful to say."

Kiedron turned to leave when Stockton stopped him.

"One more thing, sir," Bill said. "At the time of the murder, the security camera was disabled."

"That's disappointing," Kiedron nodded for Jaq to follow and walked out to the waiting woman. She was short and heavyset, with a mass of unruly black hair which she unsuccessfully tried to tame into a ponytail. He was informed her name was Alba Rodrigues. As he approached her, he noticed she was weeping quietly.

"Ms. Rodrigues?" She nodded. "Please tell me how you found the body."

She took a deep breath, then exhaled loudly. "I came here this morning to get the house ready for the staging later today, and the open house tomorrow. I always do that, used to do that, for Mr. Chepstow. Every house he flipped I cleaned, for the last 5 years. It was a steady job. He paid ok, but I didn't have to worry that he would shaft me and 'forget' to pay. Where will I find another client like that?" She reached into her pocket, pulled out a kleenex of dubious cleanliness, and blew her nose.

"What time did you get here?" asked Jaq.

"It was maybe 7 am or so."

"Please continue," urged Kiedron.

"Not much more to say," Alba mumbled. "The key was in the lockbox, as was always with Mr. Chepstow. The same combination, for the last 5 years. All other builders always use 1234, and he was smart, he used 2580, all the numbers in the middle."

Kiedron looked at the keypad of the lockbox. It was the kind of lockbox that realtors use to keep the keys in, so buyers can come in with their own realtor, but others couldn't get in. It was an older one, not electronic like most realtors use these days but one with actual keys you pressed. The numbers were arranged in 3 rows, and the middle keys in each row indeed spelled 2580. Kiedron wondered if he would ever find this piece of trivia useful.

"Why was it smart?" Jaq was curious.

Alba smiled. "Well, if everybody uses the same code, then it's just as well as keep the door wide open. But with Mr. Chepstow, you needed to know the combination before you could open the lockbox and get in."

"How many people knew the combination?" Kiedron asked. He was painfully aware that each of these people now became a suspect.

"Anyone that needed in. All the tradespeople, anyone that needed to do work on the inside. The realtor, and me. And then the stagers, they were supposed to get the staging done today. Oh, and Mrs. Chepstow. She would come sometimes to see progress."

"Was it locked when you got there?" asked Jaq.

"Yes, everything looked normal," Alba confirmed.

Kiedron nodded, then glanced at Jaq to see if she had further questions. Her forehead was wrinkled with an expression of deep thought, but she didn't look like she wanted to ask more questions. There was nothing else to gain from staying here. He gathered his team.

"Okay team. You will split and canvass the neighborhood. Maybe someone has seen something. And people have security cameras, see if you can find some footage we can use. Ashfield and I are going to talk to the family. Let's go!"

Informing the family of the death of their loved ones was the part of the job that Kiedron always dreaded. Knocking on the door of this posh Dragon Ridge house wasn't going to be any different. Jaq would be no help, as she already hated this even more than he did.

On their way, Kiedron and Jaq stopped for a moment to admire the surroundings. Dragon Ridge was a new exclusive community within MacDonald Ranch, which was already very high-end. It was located on the south end of the Las Vegas Valley, in South Henderson, hugging a mountain. To get in, Kiedron had to show his badge to a security guard at the entrance. The landscaping was lush and tropical, which must use a ton of water in the desert.

The higher up the mountain you went, the larger and more beautiful the houses became. Driving up the winding road, they admired the view of the entire Las Vegas Valley and the surrounding mountains, including Mt Charleston to the left, the only one with a snow cap. Straight ahead was the Strip, now baking in the sunshine, and a little bit further they could see downtown. This was the kind of neighborhood where you would expect to see casino executives, Las Vegas Golden Knights hockey players, and the ambulance chaser lawyers living. At the moment, they were not out and about though.

"The higher you go, the cooler it is in summer," Jaq remarked. "On the hottest summer day, it will be good 10 degrees cooler here than in the valley."

Kiedron nodded. This was going to be his first summer in Las Vegas, and he wasn't quite sure what to expect. He knew it would be hot, but it's one thing to know intellectually, experiencing it would be quite another.

All the houses here were brand new, and there were still some building lots waiting for the construction to start. All houses boasted beautiful modern design with clean lines and lots of windows.

They finally arrived and parked in a wide driveway in front of a house that would look huge anywhere else. Here it looked average size. Kiedron knocked on the door. It opened almost immediately. The woman in the doorway was tall, thin, and pale. She looked to be in about her mid-30s, had chin-length black hair, and large brown tired-looking eyes.

"Mrs. Chepstow? I'm lt Kiedron. This is detective Ashfield, Las Vegas Metropolitan Police Department. May we come in?"

The woman scanned their faces anxiously. "Yes. I'm Aubra Chepstow. It's about David, isn't it? Where is he? I called all the hospitals. What happened?"

Kiedron nodded. "We need to talk to you," he said simply.

"David?" another woman's voice was barely audible. Then they could hear a series of quick steps, and a short plump woman with very long black hair appeared. She gave Aubra a reassuring hug.

"This is my friend Mariana Reyes," Aubra introduced the woman.

She led them into the living room and pointed to the sofa. Kiedron and Jaq sat down, inviting both women to sit down also.

"Mrs. Chepstow, there is no easy way to say this," Kiedron began. "Your husband was found dead this morning."

She gasped. Her hand squeezed hard at the armrest of her chair. "Good God" she whispered. "How, how did he die?"

"He was murdered," Jaq said simply.

Aubra swallowed hard, blinked several times, then looked back at Kiedron. Mariana got up and started gently massaging Aubra's shoulders.

"Who would murder David?" she asked. "And why?"

Kiedron nodded. "That we will find out. But first, we need to ask you a few questions."

Aubra nodded.

"Who do you think might want David dead?" Kiedron began the questioning.

"I don't know," Aubra said slowly. She pondered for a bit. "David flips, flipped, houses. And also helps people with financing. The business attracts some unsavory characters. It's very cutthroat, and a lot of money is at stake. The pressure is high. Some people can't handle that. There might be someone that didn't like David. You need to talk to George. George Osborne, David's business partner, and our friend. He'll know more about it." Aubra finished and looked at the detectives expectantly.

"Tell them about Ayden. And Janessa," gently prompted Mariana.

"Surely you don't mean that family…" Aubra looked genuinely shocked.

"We need to know about everybody, ma'am," said Jaq.

"David has a son, Ayden. He is a poker player, and a bad one. He's always broke, always looking for a handout. And Janessa…." Aubra hesitated. "She's David's baby stepsister. They had a love-hate relationship. She's something else. Also always broke. Why can't these people keep their stuff together." Aubra took a big breath, and then slowly exhaled. "There is one more thing. You'll discover it anyway, so I might as well tell you," she said reluctantly. "David and I, we've had some marital problems. You see, David has, had, an affair, with his real estate agent and stager, Erika Dixon. When I found out, David was apologetic. We decided to work it out. He was going to break up with her. He left here yesterday to do just that," she bit her lower lip. She stopped to collect herself, then continued. "I was so happy this was over. I even bought two plane tickets to Paris last night as I was waiting for him to come home. We were going to celebrate there. I never would have thought it would end up like this…" She struggled to regain control of her emotions. A tear escaped from the corner of her eye, and she quickly wiped it with her hand. "How was he murdered?"

"He was shot," said Kiedron. The direct explanation was the best. No need to prolong the agony.

Mariana approached her and gave her a hug. "It's okay to cry. I know it's hard," she murmured.

"What time did you buy those tickets to Paris?" asked Jaq.

"I can look at my confirmation email for the exact time, but maybe 11 pm. Why?" Aubra was surprised.

"Just curious," replied Jaq vaguely. But Kiedron knew exactly why she asked. If Aubra bought the tickets after David was murdered, then that should clear her as a suspect. After all, a murderer wouldn't waste a lot of money on the trip that they knew would never happen.

"Do you own a gun?" asked Kiedron. This was a routine question in gun-related crimes.

"No," Aubra shook her head. "David does. Did. He always kept it in his car. In the glove compartment."

Jaq suddenly lifted her head, very interested. "Do you know what kind of gun it was?"

"A small one. Sorry, I can't help. I really don't know much about guns," Aubra was apologetic.

She sounded sincere. On the other hand, in any murder, a spouse is always worth looking at. Most victims are killed by someone they know. A husband or a wife need to be considered and vetted before they can be eliminated as a suspect.

"Mrs. Chepstow, would you consider allowing us to swab your hands for gunshot residue?" Kiedron needed to follow protocol. "It's standard procedure," he explained. "Any time you shoot a gun, the gun residue is deposited on the hands, and possibly on other body parts of the shooter. If, as you said, you never shot a gun last night, there won't be any residue on you and we can eliminate you as a suspect."

"You can't be serious!" Mariana jumped up, ready to protect her friend. "That's outrageous! Go and find a real murderer!"

Aubra placed her hand on Mariana's arm. "It's okay, Mariana. I have nothing to hide," she said calmly.

Jaq pulled out her kit and carefully swabbed Aubra's hands, arms, and face. She carefully collected the sample and placed it in a container for analysis.

There was nothing more to learn here. The detectives both got up, ready to leave.

"Mrs. Chepstow, I promise you, we will find your husband's murderer," Kiedron vowed solemnly.

Hungry, always hungry. Detective Bill Stockton was supposed to start canvassing the neighborhood, but he found himself focusing on his growling stomach instead. Food somehow was always on his mind one way or another. He knew he shouldn't eat so much, and sugar was the worst. But he just couldn't help himself. Sugar was his drug of choice. It could be worse, he told himself. At least it wasn't alcohol or something even stronger.

Luckily he always had something he could use. In his cruiser, there was a bag with his secret stash. He opened it, pulled out a candy bar, and stared at it. He knew he shouldn't. Even looking was dangerously challenging his self-control. Darn, this was hard. The chocolate was so tempting.

He stopped for a moment and considered his options. He could just eat this chocolate. He knew he'd enjoy it. It would make him feel more like himself, satisfied in his body and his mind, if only for a tiny moment. Or he could be strong and not eat it. He could put it away, and feel hungry but mentally victorious. He took a deep breath. Darn, this was hard.

Bill lifted the chocolate bar and took a deep sniff. It smelled so good! He slowly unwrapped the bar and considered again. There was still time to back out. The physical exam was looming, and this chocolate bar certainly didn't help. He knew he already was way behind. He'd have to work extra hard to get fit enough. The doctor told him he was dangerously close to getting diabetes. And if that happened, goodbye chocolate, goodbye soda, donuts, and all the treats he loved.

He waffled for a good few minutes. Finally, he realized he had to make a choice quickly. He had work to do, and not a lot of time. There was always work to do and not enough time. He decided he deserved a little pleasure. The diet would start later.

He lost the internal battle. He devoured the chocolate bar as if annihilating it would make it less dangerous somehow. The sugar rush came instantly. He simultaneously felt better because he wasn't so hungry anymore, and worse because he wasn't supposed to eat stuff like that. If he continued to gain weight, he wouldn't pass his physical. That would be bad. He promised himself he'd do better tomorrow. This wasn't the first time he postponed better habits until tomorrow and he was well aware of that, but it was too late right now. He pushed the bag deeper under his seat, pushed the wrapper deep into his pocket, and began his task.

Canvassing a neighborhood is a slow, methodical process. Bill started with the house next door to the right of the flip house. An old lady opened the door just a little bit and eyed him suspiciously.

"Yes?" she frowned.

"I'm detective Stockton," he introduced himself. "I'm sure you noticed the activity next door. I was wondering if you could help us out a bit."

The lady's frown deepened. "They were horrible people, them who used to live there. They damaged everything. Poured concrete into their toilet, and stuff. I was happy they were gone and this nice guy bought the house. And then I hear he lost it and this developer showed up." She sighed.

Bill nodded. He didn't want to interrupt the lady even though it was a bit hard to follow her story. From experience, he knew it was sometimes better to let people just talk, and clarify the details later. He wondered who the nice guy was, but for now, he just jotted it down. There would be time enough to dig into this later.

"The house was supposed to go on the market on Sunday. They mailed us postcards already. All the neighbors got one. I can show you." The lady opened the door all the way and motioned for Stockton to come in. He followed her into a dark living room full of old-fashioned furniture. An overstuffed sofa was covered with fraying fabric of an ugly floral pattern. A coffee table in front of it seemed to be grunting under the weight of old magazines. A heavy, dark dresser with ornate sculpting seemed too big for the room. The lady opened a drawer and rummaged through it. She pulled out a laminated postcard with a picture of the house next door.

"Look at this," she stuck the card in front of Stockton's nose. "See how much they wanted for that house? I was going to sell my house and go to a retirement community. My house will not sell well now. Not next to a murder!"

Stockton nodded and made sympathetic noises. The lady took the postcard from his hand and put it back in the drawer.

"I thought they were done last night," she continued. "I thought they had a buyer." she shook her head. She was silent for a bit.

"Why did you think they had a buyer already?" prompted Stockton.

"Oh, she looked like a buyer, perhaps. Certainly not a tradesperson. And she drove a minivan. It was so strange. A chic lady in a dowdy minivan." The older lady tried to explain but she managed to puzzle Stockton instead.

"Are you saying a woman in a minivan visited the house next door last night?" clarified the detective.

"Yes," she confirmed.

"Tell me more about her," he pushed her gently.

"Well, she was tall, skinny, had long blond hair, and her clothes looked like she had money and cared about appearances. That's why the minivan didn't fit. She didn't look like she would want a minivan."

"What time was that?" Stockton was furiously taking notes now. He always discretely recorded interviews, but he was worried that his battery was running low.

"Maybe 6, I don't remember exactly."

"Would you recognize her?" In his mind, Stockton already was planning a lineup with a suspect.

"I didn't see her face," the old lady disappointed him.

"Ok." the detective decided to move on. "What did the van look like?"

The old lady closed her eyes and focused. "It was white. The door opened by sliding." That was a start of a description, but not enough detail.

"Anything else you remember?" prompted Stockton.

The lady shook her head.

"You wouldn't happen to have a security camera?" he asked.

"Me? A security camera?" she cackled. "No, there was never a need."

"Thank you," Stockton got ready to leave. "You've been most helpful. If you remember anything else, here is my card." He handed her his card and moved on with his canvassing.

MURDERERS CAN'T LIE TO GOD

The old lady didn't have a security camera, but the neighbors across the street did. Stockton talked to them next. They weren't home at the time of the murder but were happy to share the camera footage. The white van was visible, as was a tall blond woman. But the sun was shining into the camera in an unfortunate way, and the details were blurry. Worse, the footage was incomplete, as at some point the sun was shining almost directly into the camera, making the picture illegible. Stockton collected the footage just in case but wondered how useful this would be. Maybe it could be enhanced, he wondered. He's seen some really bad pictures that the techs were able to clean up nicely.

Bill talked to several more neighbors, but he didn't learn anything new. Still, confirming what he already knew could be helpful in court, when it finally came to that. Someone saw a white van, someone else remembered a tall blonde, but nobody had any details. Nobody has seen her face, and no further security footage emerged. The only additional information that Bill was able to gather was that someone thought the license plate could have been out of state. Which state it was from? They didn't remember. Maybe California, or maybe Arizona.

Not all the neighbors were home, and Stockton carefully noted which houses were empty, so he could come back and finish his canvassing.

Kiedron sat at his computer, a cup of Starbucks coffee in his hand. The camera at the murder scene was disabled the afternoon of the murder, but that didn't necessarily mean that it was completely useless. He was interested in the comings and goings at the flip house before the murder, to learn who went there, when, and why.

He started watching from Thursday morning, the day before the murder. The images were of poor quality, but still, there was perhaps something to be learned. He sighed in frustration. The security footage was so often poor quality. Why do people buy a state-of-the-art system, and add a cheap little camera? It made them feel better because they have a security system, but when it came to collecting the actual information, it was often subpar.

The coffee was slowly going colder, as he sipped it with great pleasure. He loved his coffee, not only because of its taste but also because it was a tangible link to Seattle, one of the few he had. He missed Seattle. Las Vegas had its charms, its crazy energy, gambling, crowds, shows, and he loved that. But Seattle, with its polite people and cooler weather, and most of all the open water swimming, was where his heart was.

He moved to Las Vegas after his divorce. His ex-wife was from here and has brought his kids here with her, to be close to her family. He wanted to be closer to the kids, so he scoured job openings in the Las Vegas Metropolitan Police Department until he found one that worked for him. It took some time, but he hoped it would be worth it.

And now, he was in the same city, but he didn't see them very often. They were teenagers now, busy with their lives, too busy to see him. He was wondering if they were simply returning the favor. He was often so busy working that he had little time for his family. He missed so many important events, school recitals, sports games, even holidays. That was the main reason for his divorce. His wife couldn't take it anymore. He understood, although it still stung.

He watched the recording, time moving fast on the camera. Two guys came in carrying a kitchen countertop and stayed inside for a while, presumably installing it. Another set of people showed up with tools. Kiedron wasn't sure what they were doing, but they were some kind of workers. They left after a couple of hours. David Chepstow showed up in the afternoon and went in. Shortly after, a beat-up Ford F150 truck pulled into the driveway.

Kiedron sat up. His coffee was now gone, and he felt the full effects of caffeine. The truck clearly didn't fit with the project. It didn't seem to belong to any workers, and it certainly looked out of place in this nice neighborhood of comfortable middle-class houses. He looked on as a woman got out of the truck and looked around. Kiedron couldn't see her face very well, but he could see she was tall and skinny, with long blond hair. Her hair was the only pretty thing about her. She was wearing clothes that fit with the truck, old and drab.

Kiedron knitted his eyebrows. The woman in this beat-up truck looked drab and down on her luck. From the information he gathered earlier he knew that the woman in the van was stylish. Yet, could it be the same person? The hair looked similar.

The woman hesitated for a moment, and then went into the house. She stayed about 20 minutes. When she got out, she moved with purpose, jumped in the truck, and slammed the door. From her clenched fists, the tension in the body, and fast, aggressive steps Kiedron could clearly see that she was angry. But he still couldn't see her face. She backed the truck, nearly hitting a car that was passing by, and drove away too fast.

Shortly after that, the footage ended. Did someone disabled the camera? He wondered. If so, they must have done it remotely, because nobody approached the camera before it went dark.

Although the canvassing resulted in very little security footage from the neighbors, whatever was collected could still yield some clues. The investigators examined the footage carefully, and Kiedron even asked forensics if they could enhance it to get more details. No luck there, no useful enhancements would be possible. But now the investigators knew for sure that there was a white van that was possibly used in the murder. It was driven by a tall skinny blonde, who parked it in the driveway, went inside the house, and spent only a few minutes there. She then came out, drove David's Tesla into the garage, and closed the garage door behind her. She then drove away in the direction of the nearby casino. This gave the investigators something to go on.

It was frustrating that all the footage was bad and it was impossible to tell whether the woman in the beat-up pickup truck and the woman in the minivan was the same person. Kiedron tried displaying the footage of both women side by side and invited several other detectives to take a look. This didn't help at all. Jaq thought these were two different women. Bill wasn't sure but was also leaning that way. But two others thought this was the same woman. The fact that the poorly dressed woman was angry made her move differently, which made any comparison more difficult. The only thing that was clear to everyone was that finding the white van was key to solving this case.

Kiedron decided to send the detectives to find more footage. The neighborhood was located right next to a locals casino, and there were also other businesses nearby. Surely some camera somewhere captured this white van.

He hesitated for a moment. He was thinking he would give this job to Jaq. She was good at tasks like this one, but he started hearing grumbling about how difficult she was to deal with. This surprised him. He has never seen her as anything but professional, but one of the older detectives told him Jaq yelled at him and wouldn't share information. That didn't sound right, and as her boss, he needed to find out more.

He didn't like dealing with such issues. He was good at solving crimes. He had less interest in interpersonal problems. But, it had to be done. Well, there's no time like the present, he told himself and called her into his office.

While waiting for Jaq, Kiedron looked out the window. The dark clouds hung ominously, pregnant with rain. This wasn't the typical rainy season, but the weather matched his mood perfectly.

Jaq came by almost immediately.

"Detective Ashfield, I hear you had a disagreement with one of the detectives on our team. Can you please tell me what's all that about?" he was rarely this formal, but he didn't know what else to do.

She stood by his desk, calm on the surface, but he noticed her breathing slowed down deliberately. Deep breathing was a way to calm nerves, he knew that from his training. He noticed her tense jaw, which confirmed his observation of her mental state.

"He asked me some questions, and kept interrupting every time I tried to answer," she began, speaking slowly. "Everything I said, he tried to tell me I was wrong. I got annoyed with that, so I told him to shut up and listen to my answers or to stop asking me questions."

Kiedron took a deep breath. In his mind, he could imagine exactly how that conversation went. Jaq was like a bulldog following a scent and had no patience.

"And then what happened?"

"He started yelling at me, so I told him we would continue the conversation after he calms down. It made him even madder. I see no reason why someone should yell at me. He's not even my boss. You are my boss, and you don't yell," she pointed out.

Kiedron thought for a moment. "Hmm. It doesn't sound as bad as I feared. But that wasn't very ladylike," he said finally.

Jaq's jaw tensed even more. "Ladylike? Would you say this to anybody else on the team?"

"No," he replied, surprised and confused. "You're the only woman on the team."

"My point exactly," she stared at him intensely. Then she shrugged her shoulders. "Whatever," she mumbled. Then she turned around and started walking away.

"Jaq?" he called after her. She didn't turn around and continued walking.

Kiedron sat at his desk, deep in thought. Jaq shouldn't have been impolite to a coworker, particularly to someone who has been on the force for a lot longer than she was. Still, it wasn't okay for that coworker to yell at her. She could take it, she was tough. But why should she have to? Was she treated differently than the other detectives, he wondered. And if she was, was it because she was the youngest, or because she was a woman? Or maybe both. He promised himself he'd look into this, but soon he drowned in the hated paperwork and forgot all about it.

The task of locating more footage fell to detective Jaq Ashfield after all. She was glad for it. More work meant she didn't have to think about the incident with the coworker and the subsequent conversation with Kiedron. She knew what she was getting herself into when she accepted the job offer. There were some old school cops that she'd have to navigate. This was no worse than she expected. She'd just have to be better than she now was, better than they were. It would take time, but she'd get there. They will end up respecting her, she'll show them.

Focusing on her work was what she did best. She started with examining the online map of the area, trying to figure out the possible ways in and out of the subdivision. She found two likely routes for the van to use. She tried to think like the mysterious driver. Which route would she take? She didn't know where the woman was going after the murder, but it was likely she didn't live nearby. So perhaps she would want to reach the freeway? Jaq decided to start with that route.

There was a traffic light on the intersection just before the freeway entrance, and to Jaq's delight, there was a camera on it. Jaq reached out to the traffic control team to get any images they might have. She was shocked at how quickly they got back to her with the footage. Usually, it took days, but this time she had it in a few hours.

Next, she drove to the area. There was a casino, a bank, a gas station, and a grocery store all at or near that intersection. Jaq visited each of these businesses and obtained all footage they had from Friday afternoon and evening. She was going to visit the other route exiting the neighborhood but ran out of time. It was now late afternoon and many businesses were closed. It's not true that Las Vegas never sleeps. The Strip and downtown certainly don't, but other areas, away from the tourists, are like any other normal city. No worries, they would be open again soon, some tomorrow, which was Sunday, some the following Monday. There would still be time to go get more footage if her hunch about the freeway wasn't right.

Most people would go out on a Saturday night, meet friends, and have fun. It's tough to be alone and have nowhere to go in Las Vegas, where so many things are always happening. But Jaq wasn't tempted. She was single, she didn't have many friends, and the prospect of scanning hours and hours of security camera footage on a Saturday night didn't faze her one bit.

She bought herself dinner at a Panda Express and drove to the station. She sat down in front of her computer, ready for a night of work.

Jaq decided to begin with the information that Stockton collected from the old lady. If the van was at the flip house around 6 o'clock, then the blonde must have arrived shortly before and leave fairly soon after. How much time does one need to shoot someone? It appears that the blonde was well organized, so probably not that long. There was also some blurry footage showing the time. So Jaq started with the well-defined time window, from 5:30 to 7 pm.

She began with the footage from the casino. Several cameras showed the busy street, but the view was across a large parking lot since the casino wasn't interested in the street traffic. Still, the image quality was decent. Jaq watched carefully, slowing down the footage when a vehicle resembling a white minivan was in sight.

She sighed. This was Las Vegas, in the middle of a desert. Most vehicles here are white. This makes sense, as the merciless sun bakes the landscape all summer. A white vehicle gets hot just a tiny bit less than a darker one would. So everybody wants a white or silver car, and anyone that foolishly chooses a darker color regrets it the moment the temperatures reach 100 degrees. Finding the van might prove more difficult than Jaq thought.

Glenn Marshall picked up the plastic bag and carefully pulled out a gun. It was a Glock, nothing fancy, just a solid choice for people who want a gun for self-defense. This one was Glock 42, one of the smallest ones made. It looked barely used. Glenn carefully put the gun on his table, reached for his brush, and carefully dusted the gun for fingerprints. There weren't any. This was not unusual. You don't always find fingerprints on guns.

Next, he examined the magazine. This one had 10 rounds of ammunition, 3 of which were missing. This was consistent with the murder scene, as there were 3 bullets fired. Glenn carefully dusted the ammo for fingerprints. Here he found one. He carefully lifted it and entered it into the computer. A match came up to David Chepstow. So he was the one that loaded the gun. At this point, Glenn was almost sure that the murder weapon belonged to the victim.

The next step was to run a trace on the gun's serial number. Since ATF is the only one that has this information, Glenn submitted the request and waited. In the meantime, there was one last test Glenn needed to do. He loaded the Glock again and walked to the corner of the lab. There, he fired the gun into the water chamber. He collected the spent casing to compare against the casings from the crime scene. He placed it under the microscope to look for the telltale striations.

Each gun barrel creates a unique pattern on casings as it fires, and Glenn wanted to know if the bullet casings from the murder scene matched the casing from the bullet he just fired. If so, the casings came from the gun he was working on. As he expected there was a perfect match.

When the results came back from ATF, it was confirmed that the gun belonged to David Chepstow. Now, who fired it?

MURDERERS CAN'T LIE TO GOD

The neighborhood of Paradise Crest is not the most expensive in the Las Vegas valley, but it is very desirable nonetheless. Tucked between Flamingo Rd and Tropicana Ave east of the Strip, it's a lush tropical oasis of comfortable older homes with manicured landscaping, close to the Strip, the airport, shopping, entertainment, and anywhere else you might want to go. Its biggest claim to fame is Lonnie Hammargren's mansion. You can see the back of the mansion from the adjacent Sandhill Road, which delineates the neighborhood from the east. Lonnie was a former lieutenant governor of Nevada, and a neurosurgeon, long since retired. He spent his retirement collecting oddities of all kinds. Many had to do with Las Vegas history and delighted local historians. But many were just too odd. Nobody knew what would strike Lonnie's fancy next, so there was no telling what kind of oddity would find its home in the mansion. Lonnie, now elderly and unable to support the mansion, sold a part of it to another enthusiastic collector, but you wouldn't know it by just looking.

Depending on who you ask, the mansion is either a charming focal point for the neighborhood or a disgusting eyesore. Taking several adjacent building lots, it doesn't really have a style. Kind people call it eclectic. It is an amalgam of additions put in place over time without much consideration to what the overall result would look like. The multiple additions are necessary to host the owner's ever-expanding collection of just about anything you can think of. Movie memorabilia share space with an underground mine, and rumor has it there is even a barbershop brothel, although it's hard to imagine what that looks like. Right out front stands the Batmobile, an authentic movie prop. Some neighbors love the enthusiastic eccentric, others pray for lightning to strike the building so the surrounding property values go up. At the moment, another addition was going in at the back, further annoying the poor neighbors.

Kiedron entered the subdivision, drove past the mansion, then turned right onto a side street and parked in front of a pretty, newly remodeled house with attractive desert landscaping. Walking down a freshly paved path he wondered how much a renovation like this would cost. He knocked on the door and waited a bit. Nothing. He knocked again. A dog barked. The shrill bark of a small dog. Finally, the door opened, revealing a tall, slender woman with long blond hair, holding a little red dog that looked like a miniature fox.

The woman had been crying. Her eyes were red and puffy, yet she still managed to look attractive somehow.

"Erika Dixon?" asked Kiedron. "I'm lieutenant Kiedron, homicide."

She nodded. "I've been expecting you."

"I'm sorry for your loss," Kiedron began.

She wiped the tear from her face with the dog's ear. The dog licked her hand, and she stroked his luxurious fur. "It's so awful!" she exclaimed. "I don't know what to do now. He was such a great guy, I miss him so much."

She led him into a beautiful living room. As a part of the renovation, several interior walls were removed, which resulted in a spacious, comfortable room. To the right was a kitchen, and a large island separated it from the family room with a comfortable sectional placed in front of a TV. The TV was on, playing a really old movie. Erika picked up the remote and stopped the movie. The face of Errol Flynn filled the screen and stayed there, frozen.

"I love these old movies. I was trying to make myself feel better," she explained with a sad smile.

"Do you mind answering a few questions?" Kiedron asked politely, although they both knew that this wasn't a request. She nodded.

"How long have you been together?"

"Oh, on and off for two years now. We were good together. We met when David was looking for a real estate agent that can stage high-end houses for sale. I was doing that for him. I found him a few flips too, although I have my own real estate investors I've worked with for years. I understood him better than Aubra ever could," she wiped another tear from her eye.

"Do you own a gun?"

She froze for a moment. "Yes," she said finally. "David and I bought two identical Glocks. He kept his in the glove compartment of his car. I keep mine in a dresser in my bedroom. Why?"

Kiedron didn't answer. Instead, he asked another question. "Where were you last Friday night?"

"Here," she said quickly. "David texted me, asking me to wait for him, so I did. But he never came. I didn't know what to do," she started sobbing. The dog licked her face, and she hugged him.

"Were you here by yourself?"

"Yes, I live alone, with my dog. That was about to change. David was going to leave Aubra and move in here," she smiled sadly at the memory.

Kiedron raised his eyebrows. "I heard from multiple other sources that he was going to break up with you," he said, puzzled.

"What?! No, that's not true!" she exclaimed. "He was coming to tell me that he told Aubra it's over."

She sounded so genuine that Kiedron didn't know what to think.

It was 1:30 in the morning when Jaq pulled into her parking spot at her apartment. She managed to finally identify three white vans that looked promising on the footage. She made a note of the license plate numbers. One was from California, one from Arizona, and only one was local from Nevada. She was too tired to follow up on who owned any of these vehicles. She promised herself she'd start on this first thing in the morning. The Nevada one would be the first one to follow up on.

The night was warm. She enjoyed a gentle breeze as she walked to her building. The compound consisted of about 50 almost identical buildings, each two stories high. There were four apartments on each floor. She passed a chair in front of one of the apartments. There was a note on it, saying "Don't take my chair to jump the wall. Thank you." The wall was a few feet away, and apparently, people couldn't be bothered to walk past the building to the gate. Jaq shook her head. She was never surprised at what people did, but she was often disappointed. How sad that this person had to put a note like this. She wondered if a would-be jumper took it to heart if he even bothered reading it.

Jaq's apartment was only one bedroom. She opened the door and was struck by how lonely she suddenly felt. Usually being by herself didn't bother her. She was used to being alone a lot. When she was little, her father worked crazy hours, and her mother wasn't very interested in her once she discovered that Jaq would never be into makeup, hair, and other girly stuff. It was fine with Jaq, she would just read. Reading was an escape from loneliness and a great way to learn a little bit about a lot of subjects. She stored all those little tidbits of knowledge in her head for later use. They would come in handy now and then when she was investigating a crime and needed to identify an object or research something. Yes, there was always Google. But the more she knew, the easier it was to ask the right questions and find the answers quickly.

She entered the apartment. It was small and sparsely furnished. The living room contained only a good leather sofa, a coffee table donated by someone, and a TV. The tiny bedroom was filled with a bed and a small shelf overflowing with books. That was it. The closet was mostly empty, as she didn't care about clothes and had very few. All of them were too big for her, left over from the time when she was fat, much heavier than now. She knew the clothes didn't fit, but she hated shopping so she made do. She threw away the ones that were beyond hope and kept the ones that weren't quite falling off her. The result of the clothes purge was an almost empty closet. She got rid of a lot of other things too. If suddenly she needed to move in a hurry, it would take her no time at all to pack and go. The books would take the most time.

In the bathroom, she removed the bobby pins and let her hair loose. It hung around her face in a sad sloppy mess. She grabbed a comb and moved the hair around a bit, trying to see if she could make it look better. An unhappy face stared back at her from the mirror.

An empty apartment and a lonely life, this is how it turned out. She was young, but it didn't feel this way. She sighed. A dog would be nice. She was allergic to cats, so that wasn't an option. A dog would be a great companion, happy to see her when she came back home after a long day of work.

This wasn't the first time she thought longingly of getting a dog. But she knew it wouldn't be fair to the animal. The poor pup would be stuck home alone for hours on end, and she was too busy and too tired to take good care of one.

"Stop this," she told herself. "Get a grip, you need to eat something and go to bed."

She made herself go to the kitchen and opened the fridge. It was mostly empty. She sighed. The search of the freezer yielded a better result, a serving of onion soup. She put it in a bowl and placed it in the microwave. She sat down on her sofa for just a moment. She was asleep before the soup defrosted.

The canvassing effort was winding down and didn't yield anything more. There was only one house left that the detectives didn't get to. They tried several times, but each time there was nobody home. Now Bill Stockton tried it again, and this time, someone finally was available to talk to. An older guy opened the door ajar and peered at him suspiciously. He looked like he had been lifting weights, an enormously muscular, tall older guy with a shaved head, wearing a muscle shirt.

"Hello, I'm detective Stockton," Bill introduced himself.

"No speak English," replied the guy and tried to close the door.

Stockton tried to communicate, but it went nowhere. He was about to give up when a boy of maybe 10 or 11 showed up. He said something to the older guy, who nodded and opened the door wider.

"Grampa doesn't speak English," explained the kid.

Stockton nodded. "Can you translate? What language does he speak?"

"Polish," smiled the boy. "He came for a visit."

"I'm investigating the murder across the street. I wonder if he, or you, saw something."

"A murder?!" exclaimed the boy. Then he turned to the older guy and said something in Polish. The older guy shook his head.

"He knows nothing about no murder," the boy said.

Stockton turned to the boy. "Please translate for me. What is his name?"

"Bolek Sosnowski."

"Mr. Sosnowski, have you seen anyone coming or going to the house across the street Friday around 5 to 7 pm?"

The boy translated. Mr. Sosnowski said something, and the boy smiled and nodded vigorously.

"He said there was a white car. A woman with long white hair. About 6 pm or so."

"White hair?" Stockton wanted to make sure. So far everyone has described her as a blonde.

The boy conferred with the man for a moment. "Not really white," he corrected, "Light-colored."

"Can he describe the car and the woman a little more?"

A bit more Polish. And then, a jackpot. "He can do better than that!" exclaimed the boy.

Mr. Sosnowski reached into his pocket and pulled out his cell phone.

"My little sister was learning to ride a bike that afternoon," said the kid. "Grandpa wanted to show Grandma in Poland. He thinks the car might be in his video."

Mr. Sosnowski pushed his phone toward Stockton. He took it and looked at the screen. A little girl was riding a bike up and down the street, giggling. She was a bit wobbly, and once she even fell. But she was getting better and better. And then, she rode to the driveway of the flip house and turned around. There, on the driveway, was a white minivan. The California license plate was clearly visible. The video continued, following the girl, and ended after about 30 seconds.

"No woman," said the boy sadly.

"That's ok," smiled Stockton. "We have the van and the license plate. This should help tremendously."

"David Chepstow was an asshole," George Osborne poured himself some cognac, lifted the glass to the light, and admired the golden liquid. "You sure you don't want one?"

Kiedron shook his head. "Not on duty," he explained both for himself and for Jaq Ashfield. "But I thought you and Mr. Chepstow were friends"?

"Men like David Chepstow don't have friends," George sipped a bit of cognac, then nodded with satisfaction. "I was his lawyer, and we were business associates. We jointly owned

Cactus Real Holdings, a real estate investments company. We also played racquetball together over at the LVAC. Las Vegas Athletic Club, I mean. He was a hell of a player. Nevada state champion in his age group."

They were sitting in George's living room. The condo was in a highrise on the Strip, having the best view in town. The room was furnished more to impress than to make guests comfortable. The sofa on which Kiedron sat was particularly awkward to sit on. Perhaps the idea was to make sure that people didn't stay too long.

"Did you prepare his will?" asked Jaq, leaning forward and shifting uncomfortably in her chair.

George nodded. "Yes. There is some wealth there. Half of it goes to Aubra, although goodness knows she doesn't need it. The other half goes mostly to his son Ayden. He will lose it all at poker by the end of the year if it lasts that long. And there is a bit of money for his step-sister Janessa. It's not much, but for her, it'll be huge."

"Why do you say Aubra doesn't need it?" asked Jaq.

George smiled broadly. "She makes her own money. She runs a marketing agency for both local and LA businesses. I'm not sure but it seems she makes as much as David, or maybe even more. She's a smart cookie," he added with admiration. "I don't know what she saw in David, they were so different. Opposites attract, I guess," he shrugged.

"You mentioned you were also business partners with David?" Kiedron followed that idea next. "What kind of business?"

"Real estate. Cactus Real Holdings. We buy and renovate houses all over the valley. He managed the process. I took care of the legal part. We also loaned money for flips. Tough business, that. But the money's good." George drained the last of the cognac, put the empty glass on the table, and reached for the bottle. He poured a generous amount and sipped with pleasure.

"Why is it tough? Mrs. Chepstow mentioned some unsavory characters doing business with David," Kiedron continued the interview. "What can you tell us about that?"

George nodded. "People borrow money, and then don't have enough to repay," he explained. "We're not a charity. We must get our money back."

A shiver ran down Jaq's spine. George sounded ominous, making her think of mob tactics from long ago. The mob was gone from Las Vegas. Or was it?

"Did you know David had an affair?" asked Jaq.

"Yes. With Erika Dixon, everybody knew that. What an idiot! Having a classy wife like that, and he's into this thieving slut."

"Thieving?" Kiedron raised his eyebrows.

"Yes. She has a real estate investment business of her own. She'd find some poor moron, and convince him to buy a property, paying for it in full, cash only, of course. They'd then renovate it together, supposedly, again the investor paying for everything, and doing all the work, and then she'd sell it commission-free. They would split profits fifty-fifty. Great deal if you can find it. The investor assumes all the risks, does all the work, and she takes half of the rewards. What kind of a moron goes for a deal like that? Yet she had no shortage of willing victims. It was just as well that David finally decided to break up with her. Aubra was so happy about that as if he was worth it. She called me last night, worried about him but ecstatic that the affair was over. She even told me she bought tickets to Paris. All for nothing."

How much would a trip like that cost? Jaq wondered. Someone like Aubra would probably travel first class, stay at expensive hotels, and eat at the best restaurants. Jaq always wanted to go to Paris, but could never afford such a trip on a small police salary. She sighed. Kiedron quickly glanced at her and frowned. He then turned to George.

"What will now happen to Cactus Real Holdings?" he asked.

"Aubra now owns David's half."

"Can she run it?" asked Jaq.

George smiled. "Can she? Yes, she is more than capable. Will she? Probably not."

The main office of Cactus Real Holdings wasn't hard to find. Located in a strip mall fairly close to Green Valley Ranch in Henderson, it was identified by a large marquee on the front. Kiedron entered the comfortable reception area decorated with pictures of smiling people, likely the flippers, in front of beautifully renovated houses. A Barbie doll look-alike receptionist led him into the small office of the manager on duty.

"Aaron Jamieson," he introduced himself. He was a middle-aged man, very fit, with a tanned complexion that complemented his blue eyes. "What a terrible thing, about David."

Kiedron looked around the office. It was white, furnished in a minimalist style, with a modern-looking desk and a chair, and a round table with 4 simple leather armchairs around it. Aaron pointed to one of the armchairs and Kiedron sat down.

"I'm sorry about your loss." he began. He didn't yet know the relationship between the murder victim and this office manager, and it was always wise to start gently.

"Yeah. It was quite a shock to all of us here," Aaron sat down across the table from Kiedron. "David was the force behind Cactus. He'll be missed. I don't see George working this way, pushing this hard. George's a good lawyer and a good investor, but David practically was Cactus."

"Can you tell me how Cactus works?"

"Sure. We invest in real estate in general, but our bread and butter are flips. We run free seminars to help people learn how to flip houses. With so many popular TV shows, there's a lot of interest. It isn't that difficult, and many, many people are interested, particularly in times when the housing market soars, but you can flip anytime. We have customer investors ranging from blackjack dealers to doctors and everybody in between. Everybody wants to flip houses, and as long as the real estate market's going up, almost everybody makes money. Unless they do something goofy. We tell them what to do, and they do it. They buy a house, renovate it, and sell it. Then they pay us back the loan and pocket the profit.

The way it works is we have agents that find houses in the valley that are likely to be fixers. We then estimate roughly how much it'll cost to fix and how much they'll likely sell for when rehabbed. Most don't need that much work. A coat of paint, new cabinet doors in the kitchen, new light fixtures, maybe a new shower or something. A bit of landscaping cleanup, and it's done. It needs to look good and needs to last until the sale goes through. A house like that can be fixed very quickly, in a week or two, if you have everything lined up. The flippers can do it themselves, or we have a contracting company, our subsidiary, that can do it for them, for a fee. We offer designer services too if a first-time flipper is clueless, but most of the time the rehab is trivial and doesn't need enough work for a designer to be involved.

When the house is fixed up, we have real estate agents that we recommend for the flippers to list with. They're our own people, who understand the process well. They work on commission, and can sell these houses just like that," Aaron snapped his fingers.

"Okay, so far so good. But if you have a turnkey solution, why do you need flippers? Why don't you just do it all yourselves?" Kiedron was confused.

"Simple," smiled Aaron. "Most people can't afford to buy a house for cash. And if you want to move quickly, cash is king. Dealing with banks takes forever. And if your credit is shot, you won't get a loan for a flip. We're not talking mortgages here. Banks are suspicious of people buying flips without experience. They want you to live there because that makes their money safer. So, we offer to lend the flippers money, with interest, of course. This is called hard money, it's secured by the house they buy, and they pay us back when the house sells."

"And the interest is higher than if they borrowed from a bank?"

"Much higher. About 5 times as high, on average, sometimes more. You have to understand, most of these people can't borrow from a bank. Their credit is shot, and they don't even have enough for a down payment. They can't move ahead without us. So, hard money is the only way they can get into flipping unless they have a rich uncle or something," Aaron laughed. "Most people don't have rich uncles. So we fill the void."

"How much can they make per flip?" Kiedron was beginning to feel suspicious of this business.

"Oh, that depends." Aaron waved his hand dismissively. "It's up to them how much work they put into it, doing the work themselves versus hiring a contractor, the initial condition of the house, how long the rehab takes, how long the house sits on the market, and so on. There are many factors," he concluded vaguely.

"So they can even lose money?" Kiedron followed his suspicions.

"Oh yeah, they can, if they're stupid or unlucky." Aaron shrugged his shoulders. "We don't inspect the houses, as many are foreclosures or auction properties, and you can't get in. Our estimates are based on the average for the area. If there's a lot of damage, all bets are off."

Kiedron nodded. "How much do you make, as a company?"

"Again, that depends. If they finish quickly and sell immediately, not too much. Only the loan origination fee and a little bit of interest. But the money needs to move to make money, so that's ok. If they take a while, we obviously earn more interest." Aaron explained.

"And if they run out of money to finish the rehab?"

"Then we repo the house. Doesn't happen that often, but as lenders, we have the deed to it. So, we make money whether or not they do. Pure genius," Aaron smiled with extreme self-satisfaction.

George Osborne called this a nasty business, and Kiedron now saw why. Cactus ripped off their own customers, making money on their backs. The success of Cactus was not tied in any way to the success of its customers, the borrowers. And since they recommended quick turnarounds, the quality of the renovations would also be poor, ripping off the buyers. All for a quick buck.

"What happens to a repossessed house?"

"We finish it and sell it. By we, I mean David, usually. He was the one that understood construction the best. I don't know what we'll do now. Like that house where they found him. It was a mess when Rodney bought it. He had no clue. This was his first flip, and I doubt there'll be a second one. The plumbing was completely shot. He didn't know, so the cost shocked him. You know about Las Vegas plumbing, right?"

Kiedron shook his head. He never needed to know much about construction. Things just worked, and if they didn't, he called someone to fix it.

"In many parts of the country, the foundation lifts the house off the ground, and the mechanics, such as plumbing, electrical, and ducting, go in the basement or crawl space. If something needs to be fixed, a plumber can crawl underneath the house and fix it right there. Same if you want to relocate a bathroom or something. It can all be done from under the house. But here the ground is way too hard and hardly any house in the valley has a basement or a crawl space. Most houses in Vegas, even the very expensive ones, are built on a slab. That means when you build, you put in plumbing and electrical first, and then pour a concrete slab that covers it all. If something goes wrong, or if you simply want to move a bathroom to another location, you have to cut large chunks of the concrete foundation. That's messy and expensive. Plus, it slows down the construction."

Kiedron nodded. "Who is this Rodney?"

"Rodney Vance. Thinks himself handy, but this time he bit off more than he had stomach for. He ran out of money halfway through the construction, because he was unlucky with the plumbing. And he did most of the work himself. Took him forever too, because he did it after work. He was furious when we repo'd the house. But, business is business."

Kiedron thought for a moment. "How many houses did you repo recently?" he finally asked.

Now it was Aaron's time to think. "A few. There are always people that mess up or run into problems they can't solve. So, there are always some repos. And since people do put into it all their savings if they have any, it can get ugly sometimes. Like with Rodney. He took it really hard. Came here last week and yelled that he'll shoot us all." Aaron stopped. "Oh my god! You don't think Rodney did it?"

"That's what we want to find out. How can I find this Rodney?" Kiedron asked.

"I'm sure Lucy has his address. The receptionist."

On his way out, Kiedron stopped by the reception desk. Lucy was working on her computer, but lifted her head and smiled broadly, giving the best impression of impersonal hospitality.

"I need the address and phone number of Rodney Vance," Kiedron demanded.

"I'm sorry. We don't give out our client personal information," Lucy was still smiling, but her voice was indignant and her smile was very forced now.

"This is not a request," explained Kiedron. "It is a police matter."

Lucy gasped. "You think Rodney murdered David?" she whispered, horrified. "But then, there would be some poetic justice if he did," she mumbled to herself, but Kiedron heard it. "He's a mechanic for RTC, fixes busses for the city. Hold on, I have his info here somewhere.

The murder victim's phone was already examined for fingerprints. The analysts found nothing useful. The screen was freshly wiped, and the sides and the back had the prints of the owner on them. There was also a print from Aubra Chepstow, easily explained since as a married couple the two lived together, and touching each other's belongings happens naturally in this situation. It is also natural that life partners know each other's security codes. Aubra told the investigators David's code.

Now Tyler Rowlins turned on the phone and entered the 6-digit combination to unlock it. Armed with the data from the cellular service provider, Tyler set to work. His task was to determine David Chepstow's movements before the murder and also to see if there was any relevant communication that could help with the investigation.

Many a crime have been solved because cell towers can help pinpoint the location of a phone in use. By now most people know this and some criminals pay attention, but cell phones can still be a vital source of data. Luckily, in Tyler's experience, most criminals aren't very sophisticated. They don't know to be careful with phones, or they know but in the moment they forget. That's where Taylor's skills come in useful.

He started with the call log. He examined it backward and confirmed that the last calls came to David Chepstow after he was already dead. There were multiple calls and text messages both from Aubra and Erika. Tyler listened to messages from both women. They at first sounded puzzled, then upset, and then more and more worried. This fit, nothing unusual there. There was also a message from someone about going to a racquetball tournament in Albuquerque, and a call from George confirming a flipping seminar next week.

He moved to text messages. Again, there were messages from Aubra and Erika, and a reminder from a pharmacy to pick up a prescription. All perfectly innocent. Based on the cell tower information the calls and messages after the murder proved that David, or at least his cell phone, remained in the flip house.

Now Tyler needed to find out what was happening before the murder. The last text message David sent was to Erika. It said:

> *Checking out the house before staging, coming to your place right after that. Wait for me*

He never made it there, but it was good to know his intentions communicated in this message fit what Aubra already told the investigators. Tyler checked the tower that transmitted the message. It was near the Chepstow residence.

So David was home just before he left for the flip house, exactly as Aubra said.

Moving backward in the timeline, Tyler discovered multiple conversations with many people, both the day of the murder and the preceding days. There were calls both to and from Erika, a few to and from Aubra, and also calls to and from Cactus Real Holdings, George, the landscaper, and other business associates. There was a text exchange with Alba the cleaning lady on the afternoon of the murder, confirming her post-construction cleanup job the following morning, which was Saturday. All these communications occurred while David was moving around. For some he was at the office, others while driving, at or near the gym, others still at home. David Chepstow was one busy guy, moving around the Las Vegas valley like a whirling dervish.

Interestingly, there was a period of zero communication right after David sent the last message to Erika. He was home and then he drove to the flip house, and nothing happened on his phone until about 40 minutes later, when the phone, and presumably David, were at the flip house. David never responded to any phone call or text message after that. Taylor wondered if David was murdered during that specific period. Toward the end of it, most likely, since it would take him some time to get from his residence to the flip house.

Tyler found two more intriguing communications, although he wasn't sure of their significance. On Thursday, the day before the murder, David talked with his stepsister Janessa Wexton. This was the only communication he had with her that Taylor could find. There were no messages to or from her other than that one phone call, even though Tyler checked back several months. That in itself wasn't unusual, as the siblings weren't close. But the timing of this one phone call, just one day before the murder, was suspicious. There was no way to tell what the content of that conversation was. Tyler made a note for Kiedron to follow up on this. This might have been just a coincidence, but Tyler knew from experience that crime detectives didn't believe in coincidences. The conversation lasted just a few minutes and occurred when David was at or near the Cactus office.

The other unusual communication was a series of text messages that David Chepstow exchanged with his son Ayden over the last several days. The unusual part was that according to the phone records, the two haven't been in touch for the last several months, and now it looked like they were planning a meeting. Ayden was the one that contacted his father. It started innocently enough, Ayden asking how David was doing. This exchange happened on the previous Friday, exactly one week before the murder:

Hey dad, we haven't talked for a while. Everything ok?

If you want money don't bother

I just wanted to see you. Can I drop by?

busy right now

Then on Sunday morning, Ayden pinged David again.

Will you find some time for me today or tomorrow?

Alright lunch at Lotus of Siam noon Wed

ok

And finally, on Wednesday morning there was the last pair of texts.

Are we good for lunch today?

Yes, see you soon

That was all the messages in that conversation, and Tyler couldn't tell what it was all about. He was able to confirm that David was in the vicinity of Lotus of Siam, which was the best Thai restaurant in Las Vegas, Wednesday at noon, and spent some time there, exchanging a few text messages about preparing the flip house for the open house on Sunday. Without looking at Ayden's phone Taylor had no way of confirming that Ayden was also at Lotus of Siam, so he made a note for Kiedron about this as well.

There was nothing more to find from the cell phone at this time. Or was it? On a hunch, Tyler checked one last thing. Bingo! The hunch paid off beautifully. He was able to verify that David used his phone to disable the security camera at the flip house. Why would he do that was anyone's guess.

Although Kiedron already talked to Mariana when he told Aubra about the murder, he decided to interview her separately. In his experience, talking to a potential witness without anyone else present sometimes yielded information that wouldn't come out otherwise. He invited Jaq Ashfield to come with him to the interview and visited Mariana in her accounting office in Summerlin, where Mariana was a partner.

She invited them to her office and offered water, which both accepted. It's easy to forget that Las Vegas is a desert, but keeping hydrated keeps the brain going strong. Kiedron always accepted water.

"How long have you known the Chepstows?" Kiedron began.

"Several years. They had a different accountant before me, and I'm not sure what happened, but they needed someone else in a hurry. My partner knew George Osborne and so they came to us." Mariana told this matter of factly. "Later I became good friends with Aubra, although I never really cared much for David."

"Why is that?" asked Jaq.

"Well, for one thing, he wasn't very nice. And he cheated on her. She was devastated. I don't know what she saw in this guy. And yet, she would do anything for him. Love, I guess." She shrugged. "Aubra is not one to complain, but occasionally she needed a shoulder to cry on. It was usually my shoulder. David was rich and reasonably good-looking, although not my type. There was no shortage of women interested in him. Aubra always somehow managed to keep things going, or at least make it appear that everything was fine. But she didn't like it. I don't know if Erika was the only one, but certainly, that was the most serious. Aubra and David fought a lot. He threatened to leave her several times. Aubra was devastated. For a while it really looked like the marriage was over. And then, I saw Aubra on Thursday and suddenly she was so happy. She said that she talked to David and they decided to give the marriage another chance. He'd break up with Erika for good this time, and the two of them would work things out. He was supposed to see Erika on Friday afternoon to let her know the affair was over. And then, he never lived long enough to do that." She sniffled. "Poor Aubra. And George now might have a chance."

"George?" Kiedron raised his eyebrows. "You mean Mr. Osborne?"

"Yes," she nodded. "George was interested in Aubra ever since he met her. But she was already married to David."

Kiedron glanced at Jaq, who nodded quietly. This needed to be looked into. Lust can be a very powerful motive for murder.

"Anyway, I warned Aubra that Erika wouldn't go quietly." Mariana nodded to herself as if proven right.

Jaq raised her eyebrows. "Do you think Erika killed David?" she asked.

"I didn't say that," Mariana quickly backpedaled.

"What about the rest of the family?" asked Kiedron. "I understand that Mr. Chepstow had a son?"

"Yes, from his first marriage, Ayden. He wasn't always broke but he fell on hard times and was looking for a handout." It was clear that Mariana didn't approve. "He met with David recently, as Aubra told me. He asked for money, as usual. Not that he ever wanted to work for it. He just wanted David to give it to him."

"And David would?" asked Jaq.

"Oh no! David would perhaps hire Ayden to work for his company, Cactus Real Holdings, but he wasn't one that believed in handouts. I don't even know why Ayden bothered. He had big expenses, being a big shot gambler in the casinos. David didn't approve of that."

Kiedron nodded. He himself didn't gamble much, although gambling was available all around him at any time. He enjoyed going to casino restaurants and shows on occasion, and he would sometimes put 20 bucks into a machine, particularly when he had visitors from out of town and he was showing them around. When it was gone, that was it. But he has seen many people that gambled away their rent money. It wasn't pretty.

"Aubra also mentioned a sister." prompted Jaq gently.

"Yeah. Janessa is actually David's much younger step-sister. She always had those big plans that never amounted to anything. David helped her initially, but she blew it. Got involved with trailer trash and disappeared for a long while. Coincidentally, Aubra said that she also visited David recently all of a sudden, also asking for a handout. David sent her packing."

Finding Rodney Vance wasn't difficult. He was changing the oil in a double-decker bus at the RTC base on West Sunset Rd.

Rodney wiped his grease-stained hands with a rag. "Look, I have nothing to do with it," he said quickly. He wasn't eager to talk to Kiedron.

But Kiedron was used to that. "You were heard to threaten David Chepstow," he reminded Rodney.

Rodney put the rag away and sat down heavily on a bench, hiding his face in his grease-stained hands.

"I was angry," Rodney said flatly. "This whole real estate flipping business is a scam. The only people that really make money aren't the flippers. They're the people that lie about how easy it is, how much money you can make, that all you have to do is what they tell you. They make money off you. I was a fool for trusting them. I bought this house that they said was a foolproof way to print money. They said it was easy to fix. Buy it, they said. It will be easy, they said. They promised I would get rich, and quickly. I thought I found manna from heaven. I cashed out all my retirement savings and went for it.

"My wife at first was cautious. It was too good to be true, she worried. But then, I took her to one seminar and she got on board.

"I'm good with my hands. I can fix a lot of things. I fix them busses here. But a house is something else. I didn't know much about plumbing. I thought it'd be simple. Some pipes connected together, make sure it doesn't leak, and I'm good. How could I know that it's all buried in the slab? Have you ever tried ripping out a concrete slab? It ain't pretty. And then the electrical needed rewired. I made a mistake, failed the inspection, and then it went downhill from there.

"Every time I turn around, more things are wrong, I need more money. There was no more money. My wife pawned her jewelry but didn't get much for it. I pawned my gold watch, the last thing I got from my grampa. That paid for electrical, but then it turned out the roof was leaking. Then someone stole the AC unit. That's like eight thousand bucks! Nobody'll buy a house without air conditioning in this climate.

"I wanted to borrow more money from Cactus. They said the house isn't worth even what I paid for it. I tried to figure out other ways, but it didn't work. Finally, they took the house.

"My wife left me and took my kids with her. She moved in with her mother. Everything I worked so hard for was lost. So yeah, I did go to Cactus and lost my temper a bit. But I didn't kill David Chepstow."

Kiedron listened carefully. He now saw clearly how David Chepstow made his money and it wasn't pretty. How many more Rodney Vances were out there?

"Where were you from Friday afternoon to Saturday morning?" he asked.

"I was working Friday, until 5 pm. Went to a pub after that, with my friends from work. Honestly, I had a bit too much to drink. I don't remember exactly. They drove me home, not sure what time."

Kiedron took a mental note to check Rodney's alibi. There was nothing more to do here. He thanked Rodney and left.

The forensics lab was quiet, which was very unusual. Typically, there is a ton of activity, but this afternoon Dana Chan found herself alone with the task at hand. She opened a paper bag and carefully pulled out a single hair. This was the hair that the coroner allowed the forensics team to collect from the murder victim before they collected the body for the autopsy.

The hair was long and straight, most likely belonging to a woman, although it wasn't possible to tell just by looking. That's all right, it would become definite soon enough. Dana stretched the hair carefully and examined it more closely. It was dyed blond, and very recently, as there was no root color showing. The owner of the hair was caucasian. Asian hair is coarser, and African hair is often naturally curly.

She carefully examined both ends of the hair and was happy to find the root was still attached. The root is the source of genetic material, and without it finding the hair donor would be impossible. Here, the root was in excellent shape. Lucky, she thought. She so often had to deal with degraded samples.

DNA doesn't always fare well. It's sturdy if you store it correctly, but fragile and easily contaminated if you don't.

Dana carefully snipped off the root and collected it into a vial. She was now ready to perform the DNA analysis of the hair. This would take some time.

A single hair is all she had, and Dana was glad that's all she needed. She remembered the time where such a small sample wouldn't be enough to do any kind of analysis. She also remembered how very crude the early genetic analysis was. "We sure have come a long way," she marveled.

Ayden Chepstow looked much older than his 29 years. He had a rough ride. Only a few years ago he was on top of the world. A World Series Of Poker bracelet and the $1.8 million top prize made him feel like royalty. Parties in the best Las Vegas clubs, cool friends, golfing, poker for nosebleed stakes at Bellagio and Aria, sometimes at the Wynn. Alcohol and drugs, but not too crazy. After all, he was a poker pro now, he had a game to play, and he had to think clearly for that.

And women, out of this world. He found himself a girlfriend that looked just like a supermodel. He didn't know her well, as he discovered later. Who cares what she was thinking, she was hot! And when heads turned as they walked by, he saw envy in the eyes of other guys. Maintaining the girlfriend turned out to be expensive. Spa treatments, a dermatologist to keep her looking young, expensive clothes, hairstylists, perfume, all cost a pretty penny. And shoes and bags, who knew how expensive all this stuff was? He didn't mind. Money was a readily replenished stream, flowing freely. Whatever he spent, he replaced it with more poker winnings. It was easy to win. Rich businessmen always wanted to play with the poker elite. And maybe they were smart at business, but boy, were they stupid at poker.

He thought he made it and the good times would never end. After all, he was young, smart, and a WSOP champion. He was better than all those idiots who would never even sniff a bracelet. He had confidence in his game. He played well and ran good, a crushing combination. He staked his friends and won some money that way. He would buy half of someone, which involved putting out a little over half the buy-in money for the half of their tournament win. Or he would swap equity with people. This meant he gave them a percentage of his win in exchange for the same percentage of their win. It wasn't huge money but it diminished the variance. Life was good.

Yet, there were warning signs. His old roommate told him bad things about some of his new friends. Some allegedly were selling 150% of themselves, then losing on purpose, pocketing

50% of the buy-in. He didn't want to believe that the same smiling chill dude, his friend, would cheat his bestie.

His dad told him to invest some of his money in the family business. No way! House flipping was boring. Plus, his father was so controlling, always wanting something, always demanding better performance, always making him feel inadequate. Poker was his business and a very profitable one at that. And his friends made him feel good. Sure, they stayed at his hotel suites, ate his food, drank his alcohol, but they laughed at his jokes, and for the first time in his life he felt like he belonged. Nobody pushed him to become anything other than what he wanted to be, a world-class gambler, the envy of his friends.

How quickly it turned. High-level tournaments are expensive, not only the buy-in but also travel and hotels, all add up. He was trying to save money, always chasing that one more elusive win. One day, he found that his poker luck was no longer with him. He ran bad, really bad. He lost more money in one poker session than many people make in a year. When the money started running out, his friends disappeared. They were now hanging out with the latest big tournament winner, staying in his hotel suites, eating his food, drinking his alcohol, and laughing at his jokes. Ayden no longer belonged. His girlfriend packed her expensive shoes and bags and ran off with some software dude from California. He was surprised that he didn't even miss her. She was a pretty warm body, that's all he really knew about her.

He moved from a posh hotel suite on the strip to a fleabag motel in the boonies. The contrast between a luxurious suite and a bare dingy room couldn't be starker. But he had no choice. He still had some comps from playing a cash game, so he had food for a bit longer. He tried to stretch those for a while, but even that dried up too soon.

His former friends were still cool, still partied, now with the newest big tournament winner. Having no money, he was no longer cool. He didn't belong. Now and then someone would buy him a burger or a drink, mostly out of pity. But pity doesn't go far in poker circles. He went hungry a lot, lost a ton of weight, and looked like a ghost.

One day he lost a large pot and realized that was his rent money. He got kicked out of the cheap motel and spent the night in his car.

Desperate, he turned to his father. His dad had nothing to offer other than a harsh "I told you so". There was a lot of yelling and Aubra came over. He thought she would help but she sided with her husband.

He had to make money somehow. He started dealing drugs. Only to his friends at first, and then it kind of snowballed somehow. One day a buyer turned out to be an undercover cop. He was busted.

MURDERERS CAN'T LIE TO GOD

He spent time in jail. That was the time he didn't even want to think about. Thankfully it was over, and now he was a free man. But he was broke and alone. He tried getting back into poker, but that turned out harder than he thought it would be.

People still played poker but the craze had passed. Out of dozens of poker rooms around the Las Vegas valley, only a handful were still open, and the clientele was a lot more skilled now. The game has passed him by. Everyone knew the moves that in his day only the elite players used to know. He suspected that they even knew things that he, a WSOP champion, had no idea about. And he didn't have a bankroll to play even the cheap crapshoot tournaments on the strip where the tourists were drunk and money was still decent.

For a while, he hung out at the Strat. He could never bring himself to call it that though, as it was always Stratosphere for him. Their poker tournaments, even though some of the cheapest in town, were still too much for him, although he did take an occasional shot. But they fed the tournament players pizza, so he stayed for scraps. The pizza always arrived at 8 pm, 1 hour into the tournament, like clockwork. The tournament players ate first. The pizza was pretty basic, just tomato sauce and cheese. It was cut not into wedges but small rectangles, so it was easier to share.

The tournament players were a hungry bunch, devouring the centers like a locust plague. Often the only pieces left were the bread crusts, and occasionally even that was mostly eaten, leaving only crumbs. Still, he would grab whatever was left. Sometimes even that was gone. That meager source of food didn't last long, as the poker room management didn't like non-players to eat the food that was for paying customers. He was kicked out and asked to not come back unless he was ready to play. It didn't matter anyway, as the poker room soon closed.

Ayden's back was pressed to the wall. Feeling he had no other choice, he went to see his father. He didn't have high expectations, but somehow he was crushed when David predictably told him to get lost. So what now? He had no idea. He considered begging Aubrey for mercy. But that would be useless. He shouldn't have been so obnoxious to her when his father married her. He sighed. He knew he was in the will, although the majority of the money went to Aubra. Stupid Aubra, she didn't need it. Why do some people have everything and others have nothing? He hated the world, hated everyone in it. Well, maybe not everyone. Janessa was all right.

Four pump veinte mocha, extra hot with whipped cream from Starbucks was Kiedron's favorite indulgence. He started this as a habit when he lived in Seattle and a Starbucks was on every corner and in every mall. He even remembered the Factoria mall with 2 Starbucks locations, one on each end. Seattleites love their coffee, so both locations were always busy. There was a time when he drank so much of this mocha that he seemingly single-handedly supported the Starbucks location next to his office. He felt virtuous for cutting the amount of the sweet concoction from the usual 5 pumps to 4, but this was only a very small nod to sensibility.

The habit was good neither for his waistline nor for his wallet, so he cut down considerably to a much more reasonable occasional indulgence. If anything, the scarcity made him enjoy his coffee even more. It was easier to skip the coffee in Las Vegas. It was still easy to find a Starbucks, but there were nowhere near as many here as in Seattle.

His favorite moment was the very beginning. As he held the cup full of hot frothy goodness, he focused on the steam reaching his nostrils, promising the caffeine and chocolate delight. He always ordered it extra hot so it lasted longer. The first sip, ahh. He luxuriated in the familiar deliciousness.

Driving to his office, he took an occasional sip, being careful not to drink too fast. When he arrived, he parked the car, grabbed the cup, now half full, and headed for the office.

He sat down by his computer and navigated to the forensics reports. This was good news, the news he was expecting. First, the gun found at the murder scene was confirmed as registered to David Chepstow. The ballistics experts checked it out. The gun found by David Chepstow was the one that killed him. He was killed by his own gun. There were no fingerprints on it, and David's fingerprints were found on the unfired bullets.

The report from Tyler Rowlins about David Chepstow's phone content was very interesting. Kiedron agreed that the phone records strongly indicated the time of death. Kiedron also agreed that David's communications with Janessa and Ayden needed to be looked into.

Next, he looked at the quick result from Aubra Chepstow's swap for gunpowder residue. There wasn't any. He nodded to himself, as this was exactly as he expected.

The next report was about the single hair that was found on David's jacket when the coroner showed up. The hair was long and blond. It didn't match DNA in any database.

A single long blond hair, like Erika's. Kiedron now needed a sample, but he didn't want to alert Erika to the fact that she was a suspect. He thought for a moment, then called Jaq into his office.

"I need you to obtain a DNA sample from Erika, and I don't want her to know."

Jaq nodded. She slipped from his office and left the building.

Ever since she was a little girl Janessa wanted to be a star. She imagined countless times walking down the street while adoring fans stared at her. In her mind, she was giving autographs to smiling crowds, and adoration followed her wherever she went. She imagined red carpet events, paparazzi watching her every move, and parties with famous people.

This was not to be. She took acting and dancing classes, and she even sang a little. Against her mother's wishes, as soon as she was able she moved to LA with the idea that her life now began. It was only then that she realized how many other young women had the same idea. The town was crowded with beautiful, ambitious, talented competitors. She went to an audition after audition, but it never went anywhere.

One can only take so much rejection before doubt begins to creep in. After a particularly long and cruel string of rejections, Janessa realized that she needed a different plan. But what? She didn't have any marketable skills. She tried waitressing to support herself, and she hated it. All these guys leering, ogling, sometimes grabbing her, trying to get her to do things she didn't even want to think about. She finally decided that LA wasn't for her. But she didn't give up on the idea of stardom. She just needed to do it somewhere else.

By this time her older stepbrother David was becoming a successful businessman in Las Vegas. She had no interest in his business, but at least there would be someone that could help. Not that they were ever close. Still, Janessa packed all her belongings, which wasn't very much, and made the drive on I-15.

It was hot and miserable. What was supposed to take 4 hours took almost 7. It seemed like everyone in Orange County decided to spend that weekend in Las Vegas. Traffic was horrendous, the desert heat was hard to take even with air conditioning, as her little car struggled to keep the temperature down. Hot, sweaty, and thirsty, she was exhausted.

When she finally arrived it was dark. The road led through the desert and then down the hill. And then, from the darkness, Las Vegas suddenly appeared in all its shining glory. She loved the pool of city lights. And in the middle of it all was the Strip, colorful, magnetic, tempting. She didn't care how tired she was. She drove down the Strip, enjoying the sea of humanity oozing along both sidewalks, laughing, pointing. It was love at first sight.

And now? She still loved this place. It was exciting and beautiful. But success here proved just as elusive as in LA.

She didn't have a solid plan when she arrived. She drove to David's house, and he let her stay there for a few days. But he made it very clear she needed to do something. He lent her some money, and she found a small house for rent. She used most of the money from David to prepay the rent for 3 months.

How could she have known that the guy she paid the money to wasn't the owner of the house? He was a squatter who pocketed the money and left. The phone number she had for him was no longer working. When the actual owners of the house showed up, they kicked her out. They were decent people, and when she explained the situation they let her stay for 2 days, during which Janessa was supposed to figure out where to go. Her first stop was her brother. But David wasn't willing to help again. He called her stupid for being too trusting. She was on her own, completely alone in the strange city. She tried calling her friends in LA, but they seemed like total strangers now.

An attractive young woman always has options, and she was offered some. She rejected them all. She didn't want to use her body as a source of income. She had to think of something else, quickly. She found a job as a cocktail waitress in one of the casinos on the Strip. It wasn't immediately helpful, although it did help to know there was money coming. The problem was the sleeping arrangement. She had no money to rent anything, and sleeping in her car in a casino parking garage would never do. Security would kick her out, and she might even be banned. Sleeping in the car somewhere where it was allowed was dangerous. She wasn't worried about being robbed, she had little of value. But she could be raped or murdered, or someone could take her car, which would make her situation much worse.

And then she remembered her previous visit to Las Vegas. Most hotel pools were reserved for hotel guests only, and she had to show her card key to get in. But once in, she could stay for however long she wanted as long as the pool was open. There were lots of people around. Lifeguards and other personnel made sure it was safe. This was perfect. She walked through several hotel lobbies, stealing discarded plastic hotel card keys. She didn't need them to work. She just needed to show them at the entrance to the pool as a way to prove that she was staying in the hotel when in fact she wasn't.

It worked. She would spend days at the pool, switching from hotel to hotel so that she stayed under the radar. She would find a shady spot and sleep by the pool by day, and work as a waitress at night. As a new person, she got the least desirable shift in the middle of the night. Being nocturnal she could take advantage of graveyard specials in many casinos cafes, so food was cheap. She had enough to survive and even save some money. Her situation looked up.

And then she made a fatal mistake. She should have never gone to that party. She wanted to make friends and ended up a drug addict. All her money, the wages, the tips, disappeared into nothingness. She did something she never would dream of doing, she posed nude. The guy promised her a career in the adult industry. Janessa before meth would laugh and walk away. Janessa now said yes.

How quickly things changed! One day Janessa looked in the mirror and gasped in horror. Her teeth were now half-rotten, her face sallow, her hair lifeless and dry, her body painfully skinny. The photo shoots dried out long ago. The adult career never took off. The waitressing job was long gone. She was again friendless and penniless. People she used to know no longer recognized her.

That was her rock bottom. She quit meth on the spot. It was the hardest thing she has ever done, and it was still a struggle. She needed some support and found it in the form of another former addict, Troy Wexton. Troy was the kind of guy she would never look at pre-meth. A hipster with long hair pulled into a man bun, he always wore an oversized shirt hiding his many ugly tattoos. But his struggle with meth mirrored her own, and it was easier to be with someone that understood than completely alone. They were homeless for a while, but slowly their situation began improving.

They got married a few years after living together. They scraped together a small sum of money and bought an old travel trailer. They parked it in an RV park on Boulder Highway. Troy would do small jobs at the RV park, repairs, and such. They tried going to Fremont street and Troy would beat the back of a bucket like a drum with an old stick, and

Janessa would dance. But they weren't very good at it, so money was meager. Still, they survived somehow.

Janessa walked across the Walgreens parking lot and bent over to pick up a cigarette butt. She lit it and inhaled deeply. Smoking was one of her last vices, but she couldn't afford even that. There was very little tobacco left, so she puffed one more time and threw the butt away.

No money. That was the recurring theme all of her life. And this time, she again was in a pickle. Her RV, the one that she was so proud to call her very own home, needed work. Las Vegas sun is merciless. It's not just hot. The UV rays destroy the surfaces of vehicles, particularly those that stand in the sun year after year. And even more so if the vehicle's owner doesn't do any maintenance because of lack of money, or lack of knowledge, or both. Now the roof was in a very bad shape. So bad that from her bed she could see the stars at night. Now it wasn't so horrible. It wasn't hot yet. But it would be soon. She had to do something. And the only thing she could think of, the only source of money left to her, was David.

Finding Ayden wasn't easy. He never stayed at one place very long, moving from a motel to a friend's sofa, to a secluded park somewhere, where he and his car wouldn't be bothered. He wasn't eager to talk to the police, and never returned phone calls. He was known in most poker rooms in town, but nobody was sure where he was.

Some dealers said he was offering $100 per month for someone to allow him to sleep on their sofa. Finally, Kiedron located one taker, a former poker pro, now a poker dealer, who himself ran into some tough times, although he was able to hold things together somewhat better than Ayden could. He lived in a small apartment downtown and worked odd hours. When Kiedron and Stockton showed up, Ayden was there alone.

He opened the door reluctantly.

"I didn't murder my father," he almost yelled.

"We just want to talk," replied calmly Kiedron. "Can we come in?"

Ayden moved away from the door and motioned for them to follow.

The apartment was tiny and almost empty. There was an old sofa, a cardboard box serving as a coffee table, and an old TV on the floor. The kitchen was a part of the living room, separated from the main living area by a half wall. On the counter were a few dirty dishes, each different. A door led to a bedroom, which contained only a mattress laying on the ground. The bedding was messed up, and by the look of it hadn't been washed for the last several months. There must have been a bathroom somewhere, but it wasn't immediately clear where. Ayden Chepstow and his poker dealer friend were leading a very spartan life.

"Why don't you sit down," Ayden pointed to the sofa. He sat down on the floor, facing them, his expression defiant.

"Mr. Chepstow, we are sorry for your loss," Kiedron began. He wasn't sure if Ayden was sorry. "We need to ask you a few questions. When did you last see your father?"

"Last Thursday," he replied tersely.

"The day before the murder?" Stockton wanted to clarify.

"No, the day before that. It must have been Wednesday then. We had lunch."

"At Lotus of Siam," murmured Kiedron.

Ayden looked at him sharply. "How do you know that?"

"We saw your father's phone records," explained Kiedron.

Ayden nodded. It made sense to him. Of course, the police would check out David's phone and find the text messages arranging that lunch.

"How did it go?" asked Kiedron.

Ayden shrugged. "A normal father and son stuff, I guess. We were talking about how long we haven't been in touch. He knew I was having trouble finding a job. A convicted felon will never work in a casino. Too much money at risk. I don't blame them. There are other things to do in Las Vegas, but even then, they didn't want me. I'm damaged goods. Nobody'll stake me for poker. Nobody'll hire me. Well, my father would. You'll find it funny coming from a former poker pro and a convicted drug dealer, but that flipping business is not for me. I want people to know what they're in for. A player at a poker table knows they might lose it all. They hope they won't, but at least they're aware of the possibility. A flipper never thinks like that. He's convinced that bad stuff happens to other people. He thinks he's smarter. There are poker players like that. They never last long."

"Did you ever get any money from your father?" asked Stockton.

"You mean, other than birthdays and such? No."

"So you knew it was unlikely you'd get money this time. What was your plan?"

"I didn't have a plan. I wanted to talk to him. I haven't seen him for months."

"Why now?" pressed Stockton.

Ayden sighed in frustration. "I pay a hundred bucks to sleep on this old couch. I stay here as little as possible, per our agreement. If there's a visitor, I have to find someplace else. Not that there are many visitors. But it does happen. John has buddies that sometimes are even more down on their luck than I am. And sometimes it's hard to come up with a hundred bucks. I was hoping my father would want to help just a little. I was wrong."

Kiedron looked around, and Ayden followed his gaze. "Whose place is this?"

"John's. He's my only friend left from my high roller days. He was a dealer in the very high-stakes poker games back then. You won't believe how some players treat dealers like they aren't even human. The amount of abuse they take, it's crazy. Players blame the dealer for a bad run of cards, they yell, swear, or worse. A dealer must take it without complaining because they depend on tips for a living. John liked me because I tipped well, and never got mad at him. I gave him some poker lessons too. I used to be good, I won a bracelet, but nobody now remembers me." Ayden's voice sounded sad and resigned.

"Where were you Friday between 5 and 7 pm?" Kiedron was watching Ayden carefully.

"Here."

"Can anyone confirm that?"

"Jeez, how can anyone confirm that? Nobody wants to be here unless they absolutely have to. Look, I told you, I didn't murder my father. If I did, I'd come up with a better alibi than sitting in this dingy apartment."

Following Erika proved to be quite an undertaking. Erika drove all over town, and Jaq had a lot of trouble staying inconspicuous. Her nondescript looks proved to be a huge asset. Nobody remembers a mousy woman in bad clothes. In contrast, Erika was a shapely blonde driving a white convertible with the top pulled down. Everything about Erika was designed to be noticed. This made her easier to follow.

Erika first went to the Cactus Real Holdings office. Jaq didn't enter after her, not wanting to blow her cover. It's one thing to blend into the background when nobody knows you and nobody cares you're there. It's quite another to go to a place where it's difficult not to talk to anyone.

Jaq waited in the mall parking lot. It wasn't long until Erika left Cactus, jumped into her convertible, and drove towards downtown. Jaq followed her to the up-and-coming neighborhood that previously fell on hard times but was becoming very fashionable again. Beautiful large homes, many recently renovated, stood at a comfortable distance from each other. Most had oasis landscaping, which was beautiful but needed a lot of water. Water in Las Vegas is expensive. So only rich people have such landscaping.

Erika parked in front of a less affluent-looking house and went in. Jaq kept driving. This street didn't offer much cover, and Jaq didn't want Erika to notice that she was followed. She radioed for help and asked Bill Stockton to take over. He parked just down the street, and waited, while Jaq hid around the corner.

Erika spent about half an hour in the house, then left. Bill radioed Jaq, and she resumed her tracking. The next stop was a dry cleaner, where Erika picked up what looked like a few jackets. It was noon now, and Jaq was beginning to feel hungry. Luckily Erika drove to a Thai restaurant next.

Lotus of Siam is the best known Thai restaurant in Las Vegas and deservedly so. The surroundings are pleasant and the food is fantastic. But there is a downside. It's so successful that everybody wants to eat there. As a result, the wait time can be substantial. The restaurant's success led several of the former Lotus of Siam chefs to open their own restaurants that follow a similar model. Not all of these restaurants are as successful, but some are quite good. One such restaurant was where Erika chose to have lunch.

Jaq parked away from Erika and followed her to the restaurant. Erika was already seated and chatting with some guy when Jaq entered and sat at the end of the bar, near the restroom, trying to blend into the background. The stool was uncomfortable, but the view of the restaurant was the best possible. Plus, the proximity of the restroom offered some protection in case Jaq was discovered.

From the corner of her eye, she could see Erika having an animated conversation with the man. She couldn't hear the conversation, but from the manner they were both acting it looked like a business meeting, and a successful one at that because they were both nodding in agreement.

Jaq ordered shrimp soup, not because she loved soups but because it was the quickest dish on the menu. She prepaid so she could leave anytime without notice. After all, she wasn't sure how long the meeting would last. She quickly ate half of the soup, enough so she wasn't starving, but to have enough food left to drag it out if need be.

Erika and the guy weren't in a hurry. They ordered appetizers, then took their time eating the main dish. Finally, Jaq noticed Erika getting up from the table without saying goodbye to the guy. Bathroom break, most likely. Jaq quickly got up and dove into the restroom. She wanted to be there first, hiding in a stall. Through the gap between the door and the stall frame, she had a good view of the bathroom door and the sinks.

Erika entered the next stall, used it, and stopped to wash her hands. And then, she took a tissue out of her pocket. Jaq held her breath, trying to will Erika into leaving a sample behind. It worked. Erika cleaned her nose and then threw the tissue in the garbage. Jaq smiled to herself as Erika left the restroom.

Jaq waited a moment, and then excitedly exited her stall. The snot sample wasn't exactly a pleasant thing to deal with, but Jaq didn't think about that. She was focused on the DNA that the tissue now held. She pulled a paper bag out of her pocket, and carefully collected the sample. Her task was accomplished.

Kiedron drove down Boulder Highway trying to locate the RV park where Janessa Wexton lived. He rarely came this way and was surprised how little this place changed since he last saw it a few years ago. Las Vegas was always reinventing itself, on the Strip, the casino moguls would blow up hotels and build new ones, Downtown they would renovate the old structures and make them look new again. But here, far from rich tourist crowds, things changed very little.

Boulder Highway is sometimes called Boulder Strip. It has several casinos, the best ones located on the east side of the road. The casinos mostly serve locals, and sometimes attract savvy tourists that want casino excitement without paying huge city prices. They also accommodate tourists that can't afford even the less exorbitant downtown prices.

Both sides of Boulder Highway also boast a large number of RV parks. There are different kinds of parks. The ones associated with casinos tend to be well maintained, with good amenities, such as laundry, nice pools, showers, and dog runs. Others can be a mixed bag. As Kiedron drove along Boulder Highway, he wondered what kind of a park Janessa would choose. He had never been to an RV park. He had never even been inside an RV. Now he was beginning to realize there was a whole new world out there.

The park that Janessa stayed at was quite nice. Kiedron stopped at a small building that was hosting an office, showers, and some maintenance rooms. He asked about Janessa at the office and was directed toward the back wall of the park. The park was laid out on a rectangle and fully walled in. The RV sites along the outside walls tended to be smaller, and suitable for RVs to back in. The center consisted of groups of sites, some back in, some pull through. Each site had water, a sewer line, and a short pole with an electric outlet. This is where people plug in to provide electricity for the RV, Kiedron realized.

The park was like a little city, with good and bad parts. The pull-through islands in the middle hosted huge RVs, some bigger than many city busses, with multiple slide-outs on both sides. Many had hitches to tow cars. And the cars in front of these rigs were expensive. Kiedron now realized that some of these rigs could be more expensive than many houses.

Kiedron slowly drove past the RV mansions, toward the less extravagant vehicles. There were travel trailers and fifth wheels, some new and shiny, some old and dull. The newer ones tended to congregate together, and the older ones were relegated to farther parts of the park. At the very end, hugging the outside wall, was what Kiedron mentally dubbed a skid row. It was full of dilapidated trailers with all kinds of junk around them. It was clear that the residents were here for a long time, as many trailers had wooden porches added to them.

Kiedron wondered how some of them could be roadworthy since they looked like they have been parked and not moved again for a long time.

Kiedron searched for site numbers and found the right spot toward the very end. The RV parked here was on the small side, with a dull finish, and had a torn awning waving in the wind. There was an old wooden porch leading to the door. The railing was broken. A swatch of artificial grass in front of the porch was so threadbare that through the holes Kiedron could see gravel underneath. The windows were covered with silver screens intended to keep out the intense Las Vegas sun. The screens were in poor shape, bent, and fraying. But the worst part was the roof. Even from the outside, Kiedron could see the holes. This was a nice day, so the holes were merely ugly. But what about summer or winter? A roof like that wouldn't keep the elements out, baking or freezing the inhabitants. And if it rained, the roof offered no protection.

Kiedron climbed the two wooden steps and discovered that the bottom one was wobbly. He sighed, half feeling sorry for the people that lived here and half frustrated that they didn't take better care of their home. This living arrangement was only one tiny step above homelessness.

There was no time for further musings. Kiedron knocked on the door and waited. There was no answer. He knocked again, this time louder. Still nothing. He was about to leave when the door cracked open.

The woman was tall and painfully skinny. She had long blond hair, carefully brushed and styled. This was the only thing about her that was well taken care of. Blond hair, just like the one found on David Chepstow's jacket, noted Kiedron. And just like the woman that visited the house in the old beat-up truck the day before the murder. This woman's face was sallow, her clothes were clean but threadbare and fraying. She looked at him without curiosity.

"Janessa Wexton?" Kiedron asked.

She nodded and continued staring at him wordlessly.

"I'm lieutenant Kiedron, homicide," he introduced himself. "I need to ask you a few questions. May I come in?"

She opened the door wider and moved out of the way so he could come in. The inside didn't look much better than the outside. It was all one room, with a kitchenette and a dining table at one end and a bed at the other. The door to the left was most likely a tiny bathroom. The air stunk of cigarette smoke. The cabinet doors in the kitchenette hung on for dear life on rusty hinges. The two mugs on the kitchen table were half full of old coffee. The bed wasn't made.

"Excuse the mess," Janessa helplessly grabbed a mug from the table and moved it to the kitchen counter. As she spoke, Kiedron noticed how terrible her teeth were. Meth mouth, no doubt. But right now she appeared reasonably lucid. She removed some clothing from a dinette chair and motioned for

Kiedron to sit down. He eyed the chair suspiciously and sat on its very edge. She sat on the other chair.

"Mrs. Wexton," Kiedron started, "I'm sorry about the loss of your brother."

"Thank you, but we weren't close," she mumbled, staring at her hands.

"I understand. But you were in touch with him recently?" he prompted gently.

She looked up, surprised. "We talked on the phone on Thursday. How did you know?"

"From his phone records," Kiedron explained. "Why did you call him?"

"He called me," she said quickly.

"No, he didn't," corrected her Kiedron. "The records indicate that you initiated that phone call."

She stared at her hands again, clearly uncomfortable. "What does it matter?" she mumbled.

"We need to have the facts correct," Kiedron was getting a little impatient.

"Okay," she nodded. "I called him. Look at this place! Do you think it's fun to live like this? We've been struggling for a long time. No money for anything. Just one mishap away from homeless. And look at our roof!" she exclaimed. She was animated now, clearly passionate about her situation. "Look at it! We can't spend the summer like this! In another month it will be too hot to stay here. Our AC is barely working as it is, but with holes like this, it might as well be dead. How can we stay here? I called to ask David to meet me. He didn't want to, but he finally agreed. I asked him to come here, but he wouldn't. We met at the casino very briefly. I asked him for help with the repairs, and he wouldn't."

Kiedron considered carefully. "Which casino?" he finally asked.

"Sam's Town," she said reluctantly. "It's the closest."

"Ok," Kiedron was watching her carefully. "Are you telling me that if I go to Sam's Town and request their surveillance tapes, I will find the two of you on them?"

She winced. "No…" she said slowly.

"Let me ask again," Kiedron sounded authoritative. "Where did you meet?"

She stared at her hands again, then took a deep breath and slowly exhaled. "I went to see him in the house he was renovating. In Henderson. There probably is a security camera."

"How did you get there?" Kiedron had a good idea but wanted to confirm it.

"I have an old Ford truck."

So Kiedron's hunch was right. Janessa was the woman caught on the security camera Thursday afternoon. And now he felt uneasy. Her reluctance to tell the truth didn't make sense. So he asked her bluntly: "Why did you lie to me?"

She slowly lifted her head and looked at him. "I… I didn't want you to think I had anything to do with it. I thought you wouldn't find out I met with David. What does it matter anyway? He's dead."

"You stand to inherit some money," Kiedron pointed out.

"Really?" she looked genuinely surprised. "So now I can fix the roof," the thought made her happy. Or maybe happy wasn't the right word. It was more that she was relieved.

"I need your DNA sample," Kiedron decided on the fly. She had long blond hair, just like the one found on the murder scene. He wanted to have definite proof about her being there on the day of the murder, one way or the other. She allowed him to swab inside her mouth with no hesitation. He took the DNA sample and walked out of the trailer, grateful to smell fresh air. How can people live like this, he wondered.

It was late afternoon when Dana Chan finally could get up and stretch her legs. She'd been working all day like crazy and didn't even have time for lunch. She did a few yoga poses to make her aching body feel better. A coworker looked up from her sample and smiled. Dana smiled back. They talked about going to a yoga class many times, but they rarely managed to go to one, even though local casinos occasionally held free yoga sessions. Dana's favorite was Red Rock. A beautiful casino would sometimes offer its manicured grounds for free yoga sessions. She now realized it's been a while since she's been, and mentally made a note to try to go more often.

Forensic DNA analysis was a stressful job for two major reasons. First, there was so much to do. There was no shortage of crime scenes in Las Vegas, as it would be in any large city. A lot of these crime scenes had a biological component that needed to be analyzed, classified, described, and compared. There were only a handful of analysts in the lab, and each of them had their plate full. But the second reason was more stressful to Dana. She was always so very careful to not make a mistake. If she ever got something wrong, someone innocent could end up in jail, and a guilty person could walk free, possibly committing more crimes.

This was the part of her job that made Dana work extra hard. She didn't want a mistake like that on her conscience. The innocent people had the right to go free and the guilty ones belonged in jail. She, Dana, was a part of the process of sorting out who is who. She was only one of many people on the team, but she was very proud of what she did.

She sat down in front of her computer and pulled up results from two samples. Side by side on her screen, she placed the DNA of the hair from the Chepstow murder scene and the mucus sample of Erika Dixon. She compared the two samples in several different ways. There was a match. Dana picked up the phone and called Kiedron with the news.

The interrogation room at the police station was ugly and bare. There was a table, four uncomfortable chairs, and a large mirror. It wasn't any old mirror. If you looked from the other side, you could see inside the room without people inside knowing. All interviews with the persons of interest, police speak for suspects and information sources, were also taped for later review, just in case they said or did something that needed to be analyzed further. The camera kept rolling even when investigators weren't in the room. This way, anything the person of interest said or did from the moment they came in to the moment they left was recorded for later scrutiny.

Erika sat at the table, her head in her hands. She sighed, then shook her head.

On the other side of the mirror Kiedon, Jaq Ashfield, and Bill Stockton were watching. They were getting ready to interrogate Erika. Speaking softly, they were plotting the strategy. Kiedron would go first and be very direct. Jaq would assist. Bill would watch and listen, but not talk to Erika directly. The video recording had already started.

Kiedron took a deep breath. He always started interrogations this way, with an intense focus on the task at hand. He exhaled slowly, opened the door, and went in. Jaq followed.

"Hello Erika," he began cordially. "Remember me? I visited you to inform you about the death of David Chepstow."

Erika nodded. "Hello," it came out almost like a whisper."I don't understand why I'm here."

"This is detective Ashfield. We want to ask you a few questions," Kiedron was purposely vague. "Let's start with the timeline as you remember it. You said you were home Friday afternoon?"

"Yes," Erika nodded. "I had some work to do, I had a few new listings to post on the MLS."

"MLS? That's Multiple Listing Services?" Jaq wanted to be sure.

"Yes. Most agents post their listings there so that other agents and buyers can find the homes that are for sale," she clarified, then looked at Kiedron expectantly.

"Please continue," prompted Jaq.

"Posting a listing is not as easy as it sounds," explained Erika. "Some agents do a really bad job. They just snap a few lousy pictures with their phone, slap them on the website with a rudimentary description, or no description at all, and call it good. They think it's all it takes to sell a house. But now buyers are much more sophisticated. They want good pictures, a video walkthrough, a nice description. I always hire a professional photographer, unless the house is low-end. I have them take lots of pictures and pick the best ones for the listing. I then write a detailed description. All this takes time, sometimes lots of time. The best agents entice the potential buyers to come and see the house by making it beautiful and intriguing. That's what I was doing when David texted me."

"Was it how he usually communicated?" asked Jaq.

"Yes. Texting was always easier with David. He had no patience for chatting on the phone and often wouldn't even answer. So he texted me, asking that I stay home and wait for him."

"Okay…," Kiedron intended this as an encouragement, but Erika didn't continue.

"What did you do when you got that text message?" asked Kiedron.

"I texted him back, telling him I was working, and to come anytime." She didn't volunteer any more than she had to.

"What did you do then?"

"I continued working and waited for him," she paused, wiped a few tears from her eyes, and sighed deeply. She grabbed a lock of her hair and twisted it in her fingers. A classic self pacifying move, thought Kiedron.

When people are nervous, and can't leave the stressful situation, they use self-pacifying moves and gestures. Typical pacifiers are tapping a foot, stroking one's nose, and a slew of other gestures. These can be used by anybody. There are also gender differences. For men, it is often touching their face and throat. For women, one of the most frequently used pacifiers is playing with their hair. Kiedron always looked for these pacifiers, trying to interpret what they meant. They didn't necessarily mean a person was lying. But it almost always indicated that a person was nervous or stressed.

"You didn't leave the house?" Kiedron now watched her very carefully.

"No," she said quickly. "I didn't. David asked me to wait, so I waited," she licked her lips.

"How long did you wait?"

She thought for a moment. "Maybe until 7:30 or so. He sometimes did things unexpectedly, so I wasn't worried that he didn't come right away. But then, it got late, and I was wondering what happened."

"What did you do then?"

"I texted him several times, no response. I even called, which I rarely do. I was really worried by then. Look, I don't know why you are asking me all these questions. My dog is sitting home all alone and probably needs to pee. And you are asking me things you already know the answers for. It's like you think I killed David."

"Did you?"

"Oh God, no! Of course not!" she looked terrified.

"Did you go to the flip house Friday night?" asked Jaq.

"No, I already told you, I never left my house," she was getting impatient.

"Erika, we know you're not telling the truth. You were seen at the house." Kiedron sprang the surprise on her and watched carefully.

"That's impossible!" she insisted passionately. "I was home all evening. Someone is lying!"

"Erika, we have you on camera. You drove a white minivan and parked it on the driveway."

Erika was speechless for a moment. She shook her head vigorously. "That's impossible," she insisted. "That can't be me. I don't have a minivan, I don't need one. I would never drive one either."

"So you never saw David on Friday," Jaq half asked, half stated.

"No, I already told you that too," she looked frustrated and scared at the same time.

Kiedron nodded. "Possibly," he said jovially. "But we have one more proof that you were there. We found a hair on David's jacket. DNA analysis says it's yours."

Erika opened her mouth, but words didn't come out. She made some protesting noises, then collapsed on the table and started to cry.

Kiedron hung his towel on a rack, carefully placed his flip flops by the side of the pool, and slowly waded into the water. Swimming was his favorite exercise when he was troubled. The Las Vegas Athletic Club, LVAC, near his apartment was his favorite swimming hole. He was lucky enough that his apartment complex had a pool, but it wasn't big enough for serious swimming. Usually, there were too many people in it just soaking, and screaming kids running and jumping in. It was too crowded and too noisy. And Kiedron wasn't home often enough to worry about it anyway.

Given a choice, Kiedron would swim in open water. In Seattle, Lake Washington was his favorite swimming place. No lanes, no turns, just swim, as his favorite charity, the Park to Park swim used to put it.

He wasn't a particularly fast swimmer. Speed never really interested him that much. The distance was where it was at. Go far along the shore, far enough in to avoid the vegetation that got in the way of his strokes. There, far away from the shore but close enough to be safe from the boat traffic, was his favorite place to be. He did his best thinking this way. And when a charity swim was on, he would swim across the lake, 1.4 miles of uninterrupted swimming, one stroke after another.

But here in Las Vegas, there was no open water for him to swim. LVAC was the best he found.

He began swimming slow laps, one long methodical stroke after another. He loved the sensation of water caressing his body. He focused on breathing, slowly exhaling under the surface. One stroke, another stroke, then another. Turn around and do it again. Slowly, methodically.

The Chepstow murder case bothered him. Something wasn't right. He couldn't put his finger on it, but his mind circled around and around, as he continued swimming, one long, slow stroke after another. He mentally reviewed the evidence. Erica was a logical suspect. The motive was solid---a scorned lover couldn't stand her guy going back to his wife. There was proof that she was there. Forensics proved that the hair found on David's jacket was hers. Meticulous David would never leave home without cleaning his jacket, so the hair must have been transferred that day.

The security camera showed a tall blonde exiting the white minivan and going into the house, and later leaving the house, giving sufficient time to commit the murder. The van wasn't hers, and her face wasn't visible, but so far it all added up. And yet, Kiedron felt uneasy. What was it that didn't add up? He felt like the answer was just out of reach of his tired brain. Maybe if he stretched his thinking just a little bit more, it would come to him. This was a familiar sensation. When he felt this way, he usually was right. But still, it was very frustrating.

He didn't arrest Erika at the end of the interrogation, partly because he thought the jury would need more evidence, but partly because of this uneasy feeling. But if Erika didn't murder David, then who did? And why were they pointing fingers at Erika?

He continued swimming, trying to focus only on moving his body and breathing, not on the case. He wanted to give his tired brain a break. Alas, no such luck. He couldn't stop thinking about it, yet his thinking didn't go anywhere. Frustrated, he sped up his strokes. Faster and faster, a few laps and he was breathless. Panting heavily, he stopped at the edge of the pool. He didn't resolve anything in his mind, but he felt better.

Back in the office, Kiedron decided to catch up on paperwork. He hated it, but it was a necessary evil. Going through tedious details he approved some expenses for his subordinates and did other small administrative tasks. He was almost done when Jaq Ashfield came in.

"Do you have a moment, sir?"

He nodded. He always tried to make time for out-of-the-blue requests like that, although he had no idea what Jaq wanted.

"Did you rewatch the interrogation recording of Erika Dixon?"

Kiedron winced. Jaq's question surprised him. He was there at the interrogation, just recently, and he remembered it well. He reviewed the recording just this morning to make sure he didn't miss anything. He didn't find anything noteworthy in his review. He didn't feel he needed to see it again. Yet Jaq insisted on it. He sighed and sat down to rewatch it. She cued up the last few minutes. He watched carefully, but nothing jumped at him. The recording came to the end, and he still didn't understand why Jaq thought this was important.

"Okay," he said, confused, ready to rise from his chair. "I watched it, now what?"

"Keep watching," she said calmly.

Kiedron raised his eyebrows but stayed seated. The screen now showed Jaq and Kiedron exiting the interrogation room. The door closed. Erika stayed behind alone in the room. She was motionless for a few moments, then started crying. She sobbed, covering her face with her hands like a scared kid. And then, she looked up.

"Oh God please help me," she pleaded, "You know I didn't do it."

Jaq paused the recording. "Well?"

He stared at her.

"I think we have a wrong suspect," Jaq announced. "Even murderers don't lie to God."

Detective Bill Stockton sat down heavily at his desk and reached for an apple that was waiting for him on his desk. He weighed it in his hand, then bit into it without conviction. He hated being on a diet. Yet he knew he had to do something. His doctor's diagnosis terrified him. He was told to lose weight or else. He was put on a diet, and if that didn't help it would be pills, and eventually insulin. The vision of himself deaf, blind, and in a wheelchair, because his foot was amputated, and on dialysis, because his kidneys were failing drove home the dangerous side effects of the disease that he didn't even feel.

It sucked, but there was no use feeling sorry for himself. When he heard the diagnosis, his first thought was, why me? Why did it have to happen to him? He was young and granted, he wasn't as physically active as he should have been. But diabetes? But then he decided this didn't have to be a disaster. He could take control. He learned about eating better and decided to give it a shot. Hence the apple. Although right now what he really wanted was a donut. He sighed, looked at the apple, and took another bite.

The apple tasted surprisingly good. He devoured it as he watched the recording that Grampa Sosnowski made of his granddaughter learning to ride her bike. He saw the white minivan parked on the driveway. He watched the kid wobble on the bike, and finally, the minivan came into sufficient focus to see the license plate. He confirmed that the plate was from California, and he took down the number.

When he ran the plates, the result was a surprise. The minivan was a rental from Enterprise Rent-A-Car. Someone didn't want to use their own vehicle. Stockton felt the beginning of respect for the unknown murderer. Smart! Now, he needed to find the location the van was rented from and the person that rented it.

Finding the location proved to be straightforward. This wasn't the first time that a person of interest rented a vehicle. So Bill already knew a lot of people in the car rental business. He called his contact at the Enterprise and was told that the car was rented here in Las Vegas.

It turned out to be quite normal. Car insurance in Nevada is a lot more expensive than in California. As a result, many car rental companies register their cars in California and move them to Nevada. Stockton took a note of this, thinking it could come in useful in other investigations later. Right now, he was interested in the location where the van was rented from, and the helpful contact told him it was Boulder Highway. He also found out the name of the person that rented it, Matt Dillinger. That was unexpected. Not only was the name unfamiliar, but the renter was a man.

It was a long shot, but Stockton decided to check out this Matt Dillinger, wondering if he had a police record. There was no information on Matt Dillinger. No problem, Stockton knew what to do next. He searched the Web for the name and found a local student. This didn't fit with what they knew about the murder so far, yet here it was.

He drove to Boulder Highway and found the Enterprise car rental office. It occupied half of a small, one-story building. Fittingly for Las Vegas, the other half was a strip club called the Library. I guess someone thought it would be funny if a guy could honestly tell his wife that he spent an evening in the library.

The Enterprise office looked pretty much like any other car rental office. It had a counter with a couple of computer stations, a row of seats by the window, and a back office. When Stockton went in, there was nobody at the counter and no customers waiting. Slow day, he thought. It will be good for chatting because the clerk won't be in a hurry.

The clerk was a pretty black woman with obviously fake eyelashes. She was a little nervous to see a policeman asking her all the questions, but once she found out what it was about, she was very helpful.

"Yes, I can see we rented this vehicle out last Friday," she confirmed. "It was a very quick rental, we got it back the next morning. Actually, that's not quite accurate. We processed the return the next morning, but someone dropped it off overnight. Hold on just a sec," she made a few clicks. "Yes, it was rented by a Matt Dillinger, a Las Vegas resident."

"Are you sure?" Stockton knew the answer but wanted confirmation.

"Yes, that's correct," the clerk confirmed. "He paid with a Visa cash card and not a credit card, rather unusual. We made him take out extra insurance because of it."

"Who was the clerk that rented that van?" Stockton wanted to learn more.

"It was Josh. He's in the back, having lunch. You want to talk to him?" Stockton nodded.

The clerk gestured for Bill to sit down and disappeared into the back room. Presently Josh came out, smiling. He was a short middle-aged man with a buzz haircut. He already knew what Stockton was there for.

"I remember that man," Josh extended his hand to Stockton with a greeting. "Young kid. You know the type, a hippie."

"Can you tell me more about him?" Stockton wanted details.

"Well, they all think they're so incredibly different, but end up all looking the same. This one had on a gray beanie, a red and black plaid shirt, and jeans. You know the look."

Stockton nodded. Josh was right, there were lots of guys looking like that. "Was he nervous?"

"No. Why would he be? What did he do?" Josh was now curious.

"We aren't sure yet," Bill was reluctant to share too many details. "We want to talk to him because he might know something. Do your security cameras record when people drop off the vehicles when the office is closed?"

"Yes, they do, but I can't access that. You need to talk to the manager."

The manager wasn't there. Stockton asked for her information and made a note to follow up on the security footage on her next shift.

The girl was stuck. Nervous and unsure what to do next, she looked around helplessly.

"Say something, anything. It doesn't have to be witty if nothing funny comes to you. You must give something to your partner to work with. Silence is deadly on stage," the instructor coaxed gently.

The improv workshop was in full swing. Matt Dillinger stood in the center of the room, waiting for his partner, the new girl, to do something. Anything was better than just standing there. The instructor was right, something was better than nothing, even if it wasn't funny. But novices had to learn somewhere, so Matt waited.

He was a novice not long ago. He learned to love the improv ever since his girlfriend brought him to the first performance. Improv was fun. You never knew where the performance was going, and two people feeding off each other could create some hilarious results. Because performers said and did things on spur of a moment, no two shows were ever the same.

Of course, it wasn't always perfect. Sometimes there was no chemistry between partners, their sense of humor didn't mesh, and the performance fell flat. That was painful. The audience would just sit there, or clap politely, and Matt hated that. Even then there was something to learn from the failure and so Matt was getting better with each performance.

Being a performer had benefits too, although it didn't happen very often that he made money off his acting skills. Here in Las Vegas actors were plentiful, and getting a gig was hard. That's why Matt enrolled at UNLV. He was learning computer science so he had a solid income. Improv was always going to be a fun hobby, but relying on it for a living was financial suicide.

The easiest money he ever made at it was also the strangest. An older guy in his improv group, Cal Jones, asked him if he wanted a short gig, gave him a piece of paper with an email address on it, and told him to email his phone number to this address.

Matt didn't know Cal well but had heard about him plenty. Cal was a rarity, a successful gambler, and a world-class authority on video poker. Matt himself knew nothing about video poker, but they performed together a few times and despite a large age difference he liked Cal's sense of humor. Matt asked Cal what it was all about but Cal didn't know. He was just a messenger for someone who wanted to hire an improv actor for a small gig. Out of curiosity more than anything Matt emailed the person his phone number as instructed.

The next day a woman called. She had a low, husky voice and spoke slowly. It didn't sound natural. Matt was intrigued, so he stayed on the phone to talk with her. She said she needed his help and offered a ridiculous amount of money for less than an hour of work. It sounded too good to be true and Matt should have just hung up, but he didn't. Instead, he decided to roll with it and find out what it was all about.

The story he heard sounded like someone was playing a practical joke. The woman asked him to call a guy whose number she was providing and pretend to be a florist. Matt would tell him that he won 24 red long stem roses to be delivered to anyone he wanted within the Las Vegas valley. He was then to collect the name, the address, and the message to go with the bouquet. Finally, he was to pick up a bouquet that was paid for already at a real florist, add the note as instructed, and deliver it to the address the guy provided. Do all this and make significant bucks. The woman would also be on the line for the phone call so she could verify that Matt truly performed the service he was contracted for.

There was nothing funny or improv about it. Incredulous Matt asked why the woman wanted specifically him. She explained that as an improv actor he was good at thinking on his feet. If the conversation with the guy went in an unexpected direction, he would know how to steer it back on track. It made sense to Matt, but he still didn't know why she wanted to do that. But when he asked, she laughed and said she didn't need to explain herself. She then asked if Matt wanted the job and said he didn't need to give her an answer on the spot. She said she would call tomorrow, and hung up. He tried to call her back, but she never picked up. She texted him though, admonishing him not to ever call her again. Okay, whatever.

Matt's girlfriend's birthday was coming up and he didn't have the money to celebrate. A few bucks sure would be nice. What harm was there in delivering roses to someone? He wondered how he would be paid. He decided he wanted half the money in advance. When the woman called him back the next day, he told her that. She agreed immediately.

Matt thought he would meet her to get the money, but now things turned into a spy novel. The woman directed him to the Clark County Library on Flamingo Road.

"Your payment will be in the library at 3:30 tomorrow. Go downstairs to the periodicals section and find the latest copy of the *Backyard Poultry* magazine. The envelope with half the money will be under that magazine. Don't be late or someone else might collect your money."

"*Backyard Poultry*? Is this even a thing?"

It sounded crazy. Matt wondered about the sanity of it all. Could he just make up an address? Call a friend who'd pretend he was the guy? No, that wouldn't be right. Besides, if the woman knew the guy, she would know he called someone else. He thought about it a bit more and decided there was no harm in it, and he could take his girlfriend to a nice dinner for her birthday. This would sure surprise her, as he was always short on money.

The next day Matt showed up at the library a little early. The library on Flamingo Road was a wide adobe-colored building across the street from a nondescript mall. The facade facing the road looked like someone's idea of an ancient Egyptian tomb. There were no windows, and the only door was small and appeared to be permanently closed. Turning left, Matt drove along the side of the building, past the theater entrance, to the back. Here, facing the parking lot, was the actual front of the building. It looked a lot more inviting, with wide steps, two ramps for disabled access, and wide glass doors with narrow metal frames painted green. Matt parked his car and climbed the wide stairs.

He thought with awe that a library had its own theater. He had lived in Las Vegas for a couple of years and only now was he discovering the Clark County library system. He always thought of a library as a quiet place where you can get books and magazines. He had no idea about the rich schedule of events that the libraries hosted throughout the Las Vegas valley. He stopped by a display advertising free concerts, lectures, workshops, even an opera. In a library! He decided to check it out in more detail later. Maybe even he could invite his girlfriend to a guitar concert later in the week. That would be fun. And free!

Now wasn't the time to think about it though. He had a task to do. He walked past the rows of shelves filled with books and then down the narrow stairway to the periodicals section. Straight ahead was an international room. That's not where *Backyard Poultry* would be if indeed there even was such a magazine. He turned left and entered the room full of desks. Each desk had a small chair and a long narrow lamp above it so the readers could have as much light as they wanted without bothering other patrons. Matt looked around and located the magazine. It was in pristine condition, proof that nobody read it yet.

Matt didn't pick it up immediately. Instead, he found an empty chair, sat down, and waited. He positioned himself so that the *Backyard Poultry* magazine was in his full view. This way he could see anyone touching it.

There were a few other people in the periodicals room, browsing magazines, or whispering. He was hoping that someone would approach the magazine rack and place the money, but nothing happened. At 3:45, Matt got up from his chair, walked to the shelf, and picked up the magazine. Stuck between the pages was a sealed envelope with his name on it. He looked around and saw nothing unusual. People were browsing magazines, the same as before. Someone must have delivered the envelope before Matt showed up at the library. Strange. He picked up the envelope, rushed out of the library, and ran to his car.

Once in the car, he tore the envelope open and found a stack of crisp twenties. Sweet! For a moment, he considered just keeping the money and not calling the guy. But the prospect of another sum was convincing enough. And then he noticed something else in the envelope. It was a card with a florist name on it, Sweet Blossoms. It was the kind of card that people write messages on.

His phone rang. Matt looked around, not quite sure what he was hoping for. The woman knew he picked up the money, so she must be around here somewhere. But he couldn't see any trace of her. He felt uneasy, exposed. Someone he didn't know watched him without his knowledge, and it felt creepy.

"Happy?" it was the mysterious woman. He certainly was happy with the money. They agreed that the phone call would happen the next day. He would ask for a message to write on the card and deliver it with the bouquet.

He couldn't sleep that night. He was tossing and turning, wondering what he got himself into. The creepy feeling he had earlier in the library was still with him. He tried to reassure himself, thinking about it logically. Certainly, nothing he was about to do was illegal. It might be immoral to pretend he was someone that he wasn't. Could he get in trouble? Why would the woman do this? He racked his brain trying to figure it out. Now it didn't feel like this was a practical joke. Finally, Matt decided there was no reason to feel bad. He would just do it. Relieved, he went to sleep.

The next morning Matt woke up very late and was quite a bit nervous. Right after he opened his eyes, the first thing he saw was a text message on his phone. "Don't let me down" was all it said. It didn't make him feel better. But he resolved he would do it, so he would stick with the plan. He took a deep breath and texted back, "I'm ready."

His phone rang. "Let's roll," said the woman and hung up.

Matt carefully dialed the man's phone number.

"Hello?" the man's voice sounded impatient.

"Hi! This is Matt from Sweet Blossoms Las Vegas. You just won 24 beautiful red long stem roses!"

"I don't want roses! What do I do with them?" now the voice was even more impatient.

"You can send them to anyone you want within the valley, for free," said Matt quickly. He tried to sound enthusiastic but wasn't sure how effective he was.

"How did I win them?" the voice on the phone was suspicious.

"You dropped your business card in our drawing drum," improvised Matt. He waited for a moment. "You, or someone in your office," he added, sensing that he was about to lose the guy.

"Okay," the man hesitated for a moment, "how much will it cost me?"

"Nothing! They are free, you won them. We are doing it as a promotion for our new business." Matt was now feeling more confident. He hasn't lost the guy yet, which is what he was most afraid of. He didn't know what he would do if the guy hung up. But he didn't, thank goodness. People are greedy. They always want something for free. "So," he continued, "who do you want to send them to?"

"Erika," said the voice after a moment of hesitation. "Erika Dixon, the address is in Paradise Crest."

Matt carefully wrote down the address. Now the final part.

"What message do you want us to give Erika?"

The man thought for a bit. "Hmm. Oh, I've got it. Last night was fantastic. Can't wait to see you again."

Matt smiled. There was one more thing to find out. "How do you want to sign the message?" he asked.

"Flynn."

"Can you spell that?"

"F-L-Y-N-N."

Matt repeated the message to make sure he got it right. "Yes sir, we will send the flowers today. Thank you!" He hung up, relieved.

"And?" the text message almost immediately. Matt described the conversation in as much detail as humanly possible.

"Good job! Now go to the flower shop at this link, pick up the roses, add the note, and deliver it."

"What about my money?" Matt texted back.

"Deliver the flowers. Take a picture of the house and text it to me. I will tell you about the money then."

Matt did as he was told. He wrote the message on the card exactly as instructed. He then drove to an actual florist and asked for the flowers. The beautiful bouquet of roses was waiting for him, paid for already. He picked it up, added the card, and drove to Paradise Crest. He took the picture of the house first, worried that the inhabitant could watch him leave, but he didn't need to worry. There was nobody home. All he heard was a shrill bark of a small dog. He left the flowers at the door, took another picture, and texted it to his mystery woman.

"Money is in the same place," the woman texted. Matt drove to the library and picked up the rest of his payment. If only all his jobs were so easy!

If Matt thought his flower delivery errand was the last he heard from the woman, he was wrong. He received a message just a couple of days later. "Want more money?" it said. Sure, a student could always use some. He was curious what the assignment would be this time. He only knew it would be unexpected.

It was. The woman instructed him to reserve the entire Friday afternoon and evening. To Matt's delight, the pay went up accordingly. He was first to go pick up a Visa debit card from the *Backyard Poultry* magazine in the library, use it to rent a car in his name, and await further instructions. She didn't care what the car was as long as it wasn't flashy. That was simple enough, but not knowing what to do next bothered Matt. What if she asked him to do something he wasn't ready to do? He decided that if there was any danger to him, he would back out. But for now, he went online and tried finding a car.

A Friday afternoon of a busy weekend is not the best time to try to rent a car in Las Vegas. There are no good deals, as the rental companies jack up the prices because the tourists will pay. Matt didn't care about the price, because it wasn't his money. But he ran into a snag. All the cars were rented. He looked at the economy, mid-size, and even the luxury ones. And the luxury cars are of course flashy, so that wouldn't do. The only thing he could rent that kind of made sense was a minivan. The alternative was a sports car, but that went against his instructions.

He texted the woman with the news. She wasn't happy, but there wasn't much choice. Matt arranged for a minivan and asked his friend to drop him off at the rental place. It took some verbal acrobatics to not explain to the friend too much about what he was doing. As a result, Matt was slightly stressed when he arrived at the rental office.

Because Matt used a debit card and not a credit card, the rental company made him take additional insurance and placed a larger hold on his card. Matt was awfully glad it wasn't his money. He had an uneasy feeling about this whole adventure, wondering again what he got himself into. But the woman promised to pay him so much money that he just couldn't refuse.

He picked up the car at the office, trying to behave as normally as he could. He suspected he wasn't entirely successful, but that couldn't be helped. He was glad for his improv background, so he could hide his nervousness. He asked the clerk whether there was any chance for another vehicle, but they were out of just about anything other than exotics, and if he wanted one, he would have to go to the strip. The white van it was.

He drove out of the parking lot and texted the woman. The response came immediately. He was instructed to drive the van to the Green Valley Ranch casino in Henderson, and leave it at the top level of the parking garage. He was to leave the keys under the mat on the driver's side and leave the car unlocked. She then asked him to take a picture of the license plate and text it to her. When done, he was to go inside the casino, find the players club, and text the woman when he got there.

Matt followed the instructions. He drove to Henderson, found the Green Valley Ranch casino, and drove up the ramp to the top level of the garage. He had never been there and was surprised to see that the casino looked like an oversized Mediterranean villa. It had a tiled roof, arched windows, and brownish stucco walls. How little he knew about the city that he called home.

He parked the van and carefully looked around to find the woman. But there was no woman. There was only an old guy walking to his car, a group of giggling young women, and an elderly couple.

Matt placed the key fob under the mat and slammed the door shut a little too strongly. Easy, he told himself. Relax. It will be fine.

He walked across the parking lot to the casino door and pulled the handle. The smell that hit his nostrils was like a flowery soap. He read somewhere that each casino has its own designer scent. This one was very distinct. Matt couldn't decide if he liked it.

It took a moment for his eyes to get used to the relative darkness inside. He looked around, not sure where the players club was. It proved easy to find. Matt walked with purpose, passing slot players fixated on their screens. When he arrived, he pulled out his phone and texted his mysterious boss.

Here

He waited for the response for a few moments.

. Amuse yourself for a while. Don't go far

Matt didn't gamble. He never had the money until now. But the pay for this little gig was insane. So, he pulled out a twenty, found a machine he liked, and carefully put the banknote into the slot. He didn't expect much, but he pressed the Play button, feeling slightly naughty. The icons on the screen started spinning. The machine took $1.50 from his twenty, and then he excitedly discovered that he won. The excitement was short-lived. He won 75 cents, not even enough to cover the cost of his spin. Some win, he thought bitterly. He pressed the button again. And then again, and again. He won a few cents, lost some, going up and down, up and down. It wasn't that exciting. But he had nothing better to do, so he sat there until all his money was gone. He didn't feel tempted to put more money in. He discovered he'd never be a gambler, not on slots anyway.

The entire play took him about 20 minutes. He now needed to decide what to do next. He couldn't go anywhere else, because his instructions forbade it. And even if he wanted to leave he had no way to go anywhere. The woman most likely took the van. So he decided to explore the casino.

It was nice. In addition to slots, there were tables with people sitting around and betting on cards and dice. Some looked excited, others were downright depressed. Most of them were older than him, some much older. He continued walking around and found a buffet. It was popular judging by the length of the line. And it wasn't dinner time yet. Past the buffet, there was a cafe, almost empty. He checked out the cakes at the front, thinking he could bring his girlfriend for a treat. This place was nice, much nicer than he imagined.

Matt passed the cafe, and then turned left and walked a little farther. On the right, he found the poker room. He peered inside with some curiosity. It was spacious, with generous space around brown tables. Many tables were full of players. The chairs were cushy, designed to keep them playing. Matt saw some poker on TV, and it looked interesting. He now watched live people play and that was a lot less fun than a TV show. On TV they tell you what cards players hold, and you can root for them to hit the right card. Here, he couldn't figure out who was holding what. He got bored quickly and decided to continue his exploration of the casino.

Next to the poker room was a seafood restaurant, and then a sportsbook. This was a place for him to relax, he decided. There were several huge screens, each showing a different sports event or a horse race. He sat down at the back of the room and started watching a hockey game. Waiting like this was all right.

And then his mind started wandering. Where did the woman go? What did she want to do that she didn't want to use her own car? What if she wanted to do something illegal? A drug deal? No, not a drug deal, he hoped. What did he know about her? Nothing. Nothing at all. Matt mentally retraced his steps. He was at the car rental office, so they had proof that he was the one renting the van. After all, they scanned his driver's license. He also touched things in the van and left fingerprints. So, if the van gets involved in something bad, he is on the hook. Suddenly, his hair stood on end.

"What have I done?!" he chastised himself. But it was too late. His imagination went completely wild. In his mind, he saw a murderous rampage, a drug deal with massive amounts of illegal substances, a kidnapping, who knows what else. His heart was racing. He felt dizzy.

"Relax, it's only money," a man sitting on a bench next to him was sympathetic. "I sometimes bet too much too." He smiled and winked. His teeth were crooked, his baseball hat had seen better days. But his demeanor was genuinely friendly. "Take a deep breath," he instructed.

Matt obeyed. It's amazing how breathing can help when you feel a panic attack approaching. Breathing deeply, Matt forced himself to think clearly. He was in a casino full of people, with security cameras watching everyone at all times. They record it too. He could prove without a doubt that he was here all this time. He suddenly felt grateful to the woman for having him sit where he could easily prove where he was. The panic passed. The man smiled, and seeing that Matt felt better, he got up and left. Matt relaxed and refocused on the game.

I put the car back, same place

The text from the woman interrupted the final minutes of the game.

Take it back to the rental office asap

I want my money

later

Matt left the casino and trotted to where the van was waiting for him. The key fob was under the mat, as he left it. The van didn't even look like anyone used it. Maybe it was here all along? No, that didn't make sense.

The drive to Boulder Highway was uneventful. On the way, Matt texted a friend and asked for a ride back. They met up near Boulder Station and drove the last half a mile together. Matt parked the van in front of the car rental office, and jumped into the friend's car, relieved that nothing bad happened. They drove off immediately.

Bill Stockton walked into his office and sat down in front of the computer. He grabbed a bottle of water and took a generous sip. Water was all he allowed himself these days. Gone were the endless bottles of soda. He still liked the flavor but couldn't afford the sugar. The diet stuff just wasn't the same. So water it was. It was healthier this way anyway.

Las Vegas tap water is vile. It is safe to drink but tastes truly horrible. There is little you can do to make it better. Add ice maybe, so you can't taste it too well. Or squeeze a little lemon into your glass. So most people buy bottled water. Bill never used to, gulping gallons of soda a day instead. He kept telling himself it was good for him to keep hydrated. He never used to think about sugar. But now, with diabetes, he decided to be good and drink water. He started buying those huge water jugs to save money. Water was expensive. But then again, so was soda.

He stretched and began watching the video. It was the recording from the car rental company that he finally managed to get his hands on. He cued it for 6 pm. That was too early for the murderer to return the car, but he decided it's better to watch a little early than to miss something. The office closed at 5 pm, and the parking lot in front of it was empty. He fast-forwarded a bit, still empty. Around 6:30 someone dropped off a car, but it was a different vehicle. Then nothing for a while.

Bill yawned. Watching this video was about as exciting as watching paint dry. He fast-forwarded again. Wait! The camera now showed a white van. He backed it a little. On the screen, two vehicles arrived. The first one was the white van, followed by a much smaller car, also white.

The van parked in front of the office, and the other car waited. The camera clearly showed the license plate of the van. It was the same vehicle as the one in the Polish Grandpa's video of the flip house driveway. The time was 7:13 pm. Now, who drove it?

Stockton didn't need to wait long. The van door opened and a young guy jumped out. He was wearing a beanie, a plaid shirt, and jeans. Matt Dillinger, Bill concluded. He walked to the car that followed him and climbed into the passenger seat.

Bill noted the license plate of the getaway car just in case. He couldn't see the driver but the most likely scenario was a friend giving Matt a ride back home. That needed to be checked later, so he passed the information to Kiedron.

Hit! And another hit! And another! Jaq loved the powerful feeling coming from hitting a punching bag. She never actually boxed with anyone, but hitting a bag was a fantastic way to release stress. She learned that when she was an awkward teenager. She was heavy then, and looking back she couldn't believe how unhealthy she was. When stressed, she'd eat, and mostly the unhealthy stuff. When she finally decided to take matters into her own hands, she found a gym that she was comfortable with. She started with classes. As a newbie, she appreciated that someone else, a professional, told her what to do. But she quickly found classes not to be satisfying. As she progressed, classes weren't hard enough. So she took on weight lifting. A woman should be strong so she can take care of herself. Her grandmother taught her that.

Jaq hated exercising, but she loved having exercised. She loved that feeling when fresh out of the shower, she was leaving the gym tired but happy, with the satisfaction of a job well done. And for relieving stress there was nothing better than punching that bag. The bag wasn't complaining that things were too hard. It would wait there for another punch, and another, until Jaq was completely exhausted and the stress was all gone.

Dripping, Jaq stopped to catch her breath. Her hair was wet from sweat, so she removed the bobby pins and let it hang loose in a moist mess. Her face was bright red from the effort. Her sweat-drenched clothes were clinging to her body, revealing way more than she was comfortable with. She caught a glimpse of herself in the mirror and decided she looked like hell.

She showered quickly, washed her hair, and redid her tight bun even though the hair was still wet. She was deliberate in her hairstyle and fashion choices. Women have it hard enough as it is. Most of her colleagues in the police department meant well, but men were men. It was better when they didn't focus too much on her being a woman. So far it worked exactly as she planned, with a small exception here and there.

Jaq left the gym and drove towards the university. She found a small apartment building, parked her car, and walked to the apartment. The door was ajar but she knocked anyway. A young man that opened the door wore only jeans, no shirt.

"Hi!" he exclaimed, embarrassed. "Sorry, I didn't expect company." He grabbed a sleeveless shirt hanging on the back of a chair and quickly put it on.

"Matt Dillinger? I'm detective Jaq Ashfield, Las Vegas Metro Police Department," she introduced herself.

Matt turned white. Something was going on with that minivan after all. He knew it! He should have never agreed to work for the woman. No amount of money in the world was worth trouble with the police.

Jaq studied him carefully. She noticed immediately how nervous he was. She felt sorry for the dude but didn't want to put him at ease quite yet.

"I didn't do anything!" he exclaimed. "I don't even know who she was!"

"Why don't we start from the beginning," said Jaq calmly.

Matt sat heavily on a chair and told Jaq everything. How Cal Jones gave him the contact information for the mysterious woman, how he did things for her but never met her. He showed Jaq his phone with the messages, explained about the florist gig, and then about the van rental. Words poured out of him as if he was afraid Jaq would stop him. But she had no intention of stopping him. She listened, letting him speak.

Now Matt was exhausted. He poured his heart out to this policewoman, hoping she would help him somehow. When he finished, he felt really stupid. How could he, a seemingly smart guy, fall for such a strange ploy?

Jaq nodded as if she could hear his thoughts. "My next stop is Green Valley Ranch," she said. "Will I find your face in their security footage?"

Matt nodded so vigorously his neck hurt. "Yes, yes, I was there the whole time." He suddenly felt relieved, happy even.

Jaq jotted down the phone number of the mystery woman. She would check Matt's alibi later, but first, she wanted to find her.

"So you have no idea who she is, or what she looks like?" she just wanted to confirm.

"None," replied Matt firmly. "I know you think I'm stupid…"

Jaq raised her eyebrows. "You might not know who she is, but you know who does."

"Cal Jones," exclaimed Matt. "You need to talk to him."

"And where do I find him?" she asked.

"There are no improv classes at the moment, but he teaches video poker," Matt was happy to help.

Bill Stockton got up from his chair and stretched. He'd been sitting all day and sitting that long is bad for your health, as his doctor told him. They say sitting is the new smoking. He wasn't convinced it was quite so bad but his body was aching. There was one more important thing for him to check before he could take a longer break. Jaq handed him a phone number earlier, and he was supposed to find out who it belonged to.

If he was hoping for a definite answer, he was disappointed. The number belonged to a prepaid cheap phone. There was no contract. It could be traced like any other cellular device, so it was possible to know where it had been and to find the phone numbers of the devices this phone was in contact with, but it wasn't clear who it belonged to. There were ways to find out, but that would take some digging.

Bill set the phone aside. He had one more loose end to attend to. He looked up the license plate number of the car that took Matt Dillinger from the car rental after he dropped off the minivan. The car owner was Matt himself.

In Las Vegas, if you want glamour and excitement and you don't mind paying for it, you go to the Strip. If you want action at a more reasonable price, or if gritty entertainment is more your thing, you go Downtown. But the locals know that the best places to go are casinos that cater to locals. There are still a few places left where the gambling odds are decent and you have a prayer of winning something.

Not that the odds are in your favor. After all, this too is a business. But you have a fighting chance. If slots aren't your thing, there is often bingo, poker, movie theaters, and even sometimes an arena. There are multiple restaurants, and good, inexpensive buffets. They have some entertainment too, mostly directed at oldsters. But what's best about some of these casinos is video poker. There are hundreds of machines returning more than 99%. Good luck trying to find that on the Strip.

Cal Jones's video poker seminars run weekly in a lounge of one of the local's casinos. The location wasn't exactly the most conducive for learning, as the spot was in the middle of the casino floor. You could hear slot machines singing, people chatting as they walk from the garage elevators to their favorite machine or restaurant, general announcements pipe through the sound system, and overall there is lots of typical casino noise.

Cal never paid attention to any of this. He was on a mission: to help video poker players play better. Maybe not to make them all winning players. That takes hard work, and most of his students weren't this dedicated. Many would come once or twice, get discouraged that Cal is not handing out instant magical solutions and that they have to put in the hours of study.

Some students come for the entire series of classes. Of those, a subset will spend some time studying and become better. Only one or two will beat the casinos in the long run.

Cal knows studying is the key to success. There is no other way, and he doesn't hide it. The casino knows it too. In fact, the casino counts on people being lazy. After taking Cal's classes people think they're better than they really are, they go play, and they lose. This is the only reason why the casino bosses still allow Cal to teach. The false sense of knowledge that some players come out of the seminars with makes them cocky. They lose, and that pays for the scant few that do improve. And if one or two do become strong, winning players, there is always the advantage player tracking software that runs on every machine and tracks the players' every move. Good players are not that hard for casinos to identify. And once their secret is out, they are banned from playing video poker forever. Cal himself was banned from many casinos in Nevada and elsewhere. This comes with the territory.

Jaq had heard about Cal Jones before but had never met him. She also knew that some casino games are beatable, but never acted on this knowledge. She wasn't a gambler. Not that she wasn't smart enough. She knew that if she studied hard she could become proficient enough. But knowledge is one thing, being able to pull it off in practice is quite another. Having a bankroll sufficient to survive the ups and downs of gambling, while not simple to acquire, is the easier part. Having the stomach to sustain the inevitable losing streaks and still keep playing well was where Jaq suspected she would have trouble. The thought of losing more than a few bucks made her sick. Still, she was curious and was looking forward to learning more. The classes were free. What was there to lose?

Before the class started Jaq walked to the players club and got herself a player's card. It was simple. All she had to do was show her driver's license and the casino gave her a card that looked very much like a credit card. A nice lady at the players club counter told her to always insert the card into a slot in the machine and verify that the machine read it correctly before she started playing. There were rewards for players, from free buffet to expensive meals at the steak house, shows, and things that didn't interest Jaq, such as a free stay in the hotel. Who needs a hotel room when one already lives in Las Vegas? But she appreciated that out-of-town guests probably loved free rooms.

Jaq took her player's card and proceeded to the lounge. Today's seminar was about Not So Ugly deuces wild, which was a variation of video poker in which all deuces can stand for any other card. As Cal explained, this by itself is not a beatable game, but add the slot club promotions and points, and now we have a return of over 100%. When Jaq showed up, the class had just started.

Jaq signed in for the class by giving an assistant her name and the slot club card number, picked up the class handout and a bottle of water, and sat down in a lounge chair toward the back of the class.

Cal was an older guy, tall, with a head full of gray hair, and a friendly smile. He used a microphone so people in the back could hear him, and used a deck of slides projected on the screen behind him, like in an old-fashioned class or a business meeting.

Cal methodically went through the long list of strategy rules, carefully explaining the correct play for each rule, illustrating it with sample hands. He then presented the class with a series of exercises, calling on each person to give their answer. Some people got it, others squirmed uncomfortably, but Cal wasn't about to baby them. In gambling, nobody babies you. You have to make the decision and go with it. The question he now asked was particularly difficult, and he called on an unfortunate older guy who huffed and puffed, and after a solid minute of thinking was no closer to the answer than he was at the beginning.

"You must answer before the casino closes, Don." joked Cal. Of course, the casino never closes. This is where Jaq noticed that Cal used people's names. He tried very hard to remember everyone's name. This would be helpful, she smiled to herself.

As Don was thinking, Jaq tried to come up with the answer on her own. When Don finally gave his answer, it was different from hers. She got it wrong.

"He is right," proclaimed Cal. He continued the class, as Jaq listened carefully. This was a lot more complicated than she thought.

The class was coming to a close. Cal mentioned the books that he was selling and invited questions.

"If after class you have a question, you can email me. I will answer if you ask politely." The implied message was that there must have been people who were very much not polite in asking questions. This was a voluntary activity for Cal. How could people be so demanding from someone so generous, wondered Jaq? Cal probably had quite a few stories about that.

After the class, some students stayed behind to chat with Cal. Jaq waited, suddenly star-struck. Here in front of her stood a real professional gambler. Not only that, but he was hugely successful, one of the best in the world. She was amazed that a guy like that shared his knowledge freely with anyone interested, and all they needed to do was show up.

How many people learned enough to be dangerous today? Don the older guy that gave the right answer to the difficult question was a good candidate. Jaq wondered if she, a simple police officer, could learn enough to maybe make some money on the side. And then she remembered the questions Cal asked the class. They were difficult for her to follow. Perhaps if she had more time she could learn more. Right now she wasn't ready. She was here for a different reason. She needed to talk to Cal about one of his former students.

"Cal Jones? I'm detective Jaq Ashfield from Las Vegas Metropolitan Police Department. Do you have a moment?"

Cal turned to Jaq and stared at her expectantly. He didn't look very happy. As a professional gambler, he was never thrilled to talk to the police. Not that he had anything to worry about. He never hid what he did for a living. He paid his taxes like any other citizen and tried to live a life out of trouble. But you never knew with police, particularly if you were a well-known professional gambler. Police didn't understand gambling.

"We are investigating a murder," Jaq began. She intended to put him at ease, but how could this kind of opening make anyone comfortable? Outwardly calm, she was kicking herself mentally for the awkward conversation starter. After a few months on the police force, she thought herself somewhat experienced. She just discovered she had a lot to learn about interviewing people.

Cal raised his eyebrows, clearly not expecting this. "A murder? I'm afraid I can't help you. I know nothing about any murder."

"But you can still help." Jaq smiled. "You do improv comedy, don't you?"

"Yes," Cal was again surprised at the question. He didn't expect that she knew this about him. It wasn't a secret, but he didn't advertise it either. He mentioned it in class a couple of times, but that was it. And what was the connection between his improv hobby and a murder?

"I noticed that you collect the names of all the people that take your seminars." continued Jaq. "One of your participants asked you about improv recently. She wanted to hire an actor. Do you remember who that was?"

Cal nodded. Yes, he remembered. He didn't know her last name, but that should be easy to find from the records, assuming that she provided her real name. "She wanted to hire someone who could think on their feet. I don't exactly know what she needed that person to do and I never asked. But I did connect her with an actor from my improv group and I heard later that she hired him. She was a very attractive woman, easy to remember," Cal recalled. "We can look up the last name, but I remember her first name was Aubra."

It took all the inner strength for Jaq to not betray her surprise. She collected herself quickly. "What was the name of the actor?" she asked, although she already knew the answer.

"Matt Dillinger," replied Cal. "I hope Matt is not in trouble?"

"We're just ringing to rule him out," smiled Jaq. "We needed to make sure."

Cal Jones's records confirmed the student was Aubra Chepstow. She was the mystery woman who hired Matt Dillinger to find out who her husband was cheating on her with and to rent the van that she later drove to shoot David. She was the one who tried to frame Erika, and it almost worked.

Jaq drove back to the office, all excited. The mystery was solved. Now all they needed was to tie all the loose ends. They already had a lot. Game over, Aubra! Your blonde wig could fool us only for so long.

Aubra Chepstow looked in the mirror. She didn't look anywhere close to her age, thank goodness. She looked to be in her mid-thirties, not because of particular luck in the genetics lottery, or due to savvy lifestyle choices. It was true that Aubra went to the gym regularly, and tried to eat right religiously. She never smoked, was careful about alcohol, and made sure to get enough sleep. But her youthful looks were courtesy of her dermatologist, the best one in town. She was in fact 56, slightly older than David. It took several treatments combined, including botox, dermal fillers, lasers, and Ultherapy repeated periodically to look this good. That, plus spa treatments, massages, and a good haircut and color, did wonders for her appearance. With recent technology advances, looking young was simply a matter of money.

But while it was possible to cheat in the looks department, there was no cheating mother nature on other fronts. Aubra was beginning to feel little aches and pains here and there. Her body didn't recover from intense physical efforts as quickly as it used to. Her vision wasn't as clear, and her brain as sharp as it was only a few years ago. "Aging sucks," she thought. The fact was, she was tired. When the doorbell rang and she opened the door, she looked deflated. Two police officers stood there patiently.

"Do you know why we are here?" asked Kiedron.

Aubra nodded. She wasn't surprised when Kiedron and Jaq Ashfield showed up at her door. She invited them in, at peace with herself. They all sat down in the living room.

"Mrs. Chepstow, I promised you we would find your husband's killer, and we did," continued Kiedron. "You were very clever, but you made a few mistakes. We know from Matt

Dillinger that you were the one that used the white minivan he rented."

Aubra looked at him with a blank expression. "He didn't know me," she said in monotone.

"No, he didn't. But Cal Jones did. He told us your name. That was your mistake, using your own name in the video poker class."

Aubra nodded. Despite all the beauty treatments, she suddenly looked old. "He was going to leave me," she said, staring into space. "I suspected it, and when I confronted him about it, it didn't go well for me. Erika was younger, full of life. I did what I could. I found the best dermatologist in town, did all these treatments. Do you know some of them hurt like hell? And all this didn't matter," she added bitterly.

"So you decided to kill him," Jaq said. "Why not just divorce him?"

Aubra shook her head. "I couldn't let that happen. He was my husband, he belonged with me." She sat motionless, her face reflecting the pain of losing a loved one.

"There are a few things we want to clarify," Kiedron just had to ask. He had a confession, but he didn't like loose ends. "Who disabled the security camera at the flip house?"

"I did," admitted Aubra. "David came home for lunch on Friday only to tell me he was leaving me." A tear rolled down her face. "I already had everything planned. I knew all about his affair. I suspected it for some time, so I hired Matt to find out who he was with. Matt posed as a florist and David sent flowers to Erika, not to me. He had affairs before but never like this. Those things didn't matter, they were just little flings. He'd never send flowers to them because their feelings didn't matter to David. But this time I knew it was different. I had a few days to plan but had to act quickly. I bought a blond wig, so I looked like her if you weren't looking too closely. Her physique is similar to mine. That Friday he was going to the flip house and then to Erika's. It was a perfect setup, and if he moved in with her it would be too late. When he went to the bathroom, he left his phone on the table. I used it to text Erika to stay home and wait and then disabled the security camera. I didn't want David to know that I did it, so I powered the phone down. There would be no phone calls or texts to upset my plans. He was in a hurry and didn't notice. I then went to get the car that Matt rented for me, and was unhappy it was a minivan. Who drives a minivan? I'm not a soccer mom. But they didn't have anything else, can you believe it?"

"So you got the minivan, drove it to the flip house, shot David, moved his car to the garage, and then returned the van to Matt?"

"Yes. I powered up David's cell phone before I left."

"Another thing, we swabbed your hands for gunpowder residue, and it came back clean," Bill said. "And we now know you did use a gun. How did you pull that off?"

"Gloves," Aubra almost laughed. "I wore them inside the flip house and then discarded them in a garbage bin at Green Valley Ranch when I dropped off the van for Matt to return to the rental place. I knew nobody would look for them there."

"Why did you make Matt wait in the casino?" asked Jaq.

Aubra smiled. "I thought I planned things pretty well. But if they didn't go as I wanted them to, Matt was safe there. He's a good kid. I didn't want him to get tangled up in my problems. A casino has cameras everywhere. I told him to stay there so he could prove he wasn't involved."

"You're such a kind soul," Jaq mumbled sarcastically. Aubra shrugged her shoulders.

"Why did you drive David's Tesla into the garage?" asked Kiedron, although he suspected the reason already.

"I wanted to make it look like David wasn't at the house. When people went looking for him that night, I wanted to make sure there was no reason for anyone to go inside until I bought the tickets to Paris, and I didn't want to buy them too early. I wanted to be able to say that I drove past the flip house and it was empty. I knew Erika would drive past it too, and I didn't want David to be found too soon."

"That makes sense. But I don't understand one thing. How did Erika's hair end up on David's jacket? Erika never saw David that Friday." wondered Jaq.

"She planted it there, obviously," pointed out Kiedron.

"Yes, I did," admitted Aubra. "I found it on David's shirt the other day. I saved it in a clean sandwich bag, thinking I would confront him with it. But then he sent the flowers to Erika, and I knew things were a lot more serious than I thought."

"Ah, that explains the sandwich bag at the crime scene. I was bothered by it but it's quite simple," exclaimed Kiedron. "You forgot to take it with you when you planted the hair."

Aubra nodded. "Killing someone is a lot harder than I thought. I thought I had a great plan and could execute it flawlessly. I am normally pretty level-headed, but this was horrible. I made that one mistake, I left the sandwich bag by David's body, and was furious with myself about it. The other mistake was to use my own name in the video poker class. I thought I would be far enough removed from the murder that it didn't matter. After all, Matt didn't know who I was. And yet, you found me. You are smart." there was reluctant admiration in her voice.

Kiedron smiled to himself. This wasn't the first time a criminal thought they were smarter than the police. Many times he and his team caught someone truly brilliant, and the criminal was shocked to find that they actually made mistakes for the police to find. They might have been smarter than each police officer individually. But they forgot they had the entire team of dedicated experienced professionals to deal with. One person figured out one part, another one noticed something else. It's difficult to outsmart the entire team of professionals.

"Aubra Chepstow, you are under arrest for the murder of your husband David Chepstow," Kiedron made it official.

Aubra nodded. "I know. I will go with you without an incident. But I need to go to the bathroom first please."

Kiedron looked at Jaq and nodded. Jaq got up and walked to the powder room near the front of the house. She opened the door and carefully scanned the inside. There was no escape from here. The room was small and windowless, it had only a toilet and a pedestal sink in it. Just in case, Jaq bent over and looked at the floor. Nothing interesting here. Then she carefully examined the ceiling. Everything looked normal. There was no escape from here, no exit other than the door. Jaq came back to the living room and nodded at Kiedron.

"All right, Mrs. Chepstow, you may use the bathroom. But first, we need to make sure you don't have a weapon on you."

Aubra got up, and Jaq carefully patted her down. There was nothing to find. Aubra then walked to the powder room and closed the door behind her. She was there for a few moments, and then suddenly, they heard a gunshot.

"What the hell?!" exclaimed Kiedron. Both he and Jaq jumped up and came running to the powder room. The door wasn't locked. Crumpled on the floor was Aubra, dead now. A small gun fell into the sink. Jaq covered her mouth with her hand, shaking her head.

"I don't get it!" Jaq screamed, "I checked everything!"

The toilet tank was open, the lid leaning against the wall. On the floor next to it was a plastic container that was dripping wet.

"She hid the gun in the toilet tank," mumbled Kiedron in amazement and admiration.

Kiedron, Jaq Ashfield, and Bill Stockton sat around a table in the Starbucks cafe near the police station, enjoying the caffeinated treats. Or at least two of them did. As usual, Kiedron ordered his 4 pump veinte mocha extra hot with whipped cream, and carefully took the first sip. It was heaven. Jaq ordered an iced latte, and Bill just sipped water with a slice of lemon.

"You guys are crazy to pay so much for a drink that's full of sugar," was his comment. Kiedron nodded. Yes, this was an expensive habit, but the coffee was so good! And he didn't allow himself this luxury very often. Today was a celebration. But he understood Bill and his diabetes concerns. Bill was doing very well. He already lost some weight.

"So, when did you know it wasn't Erika?" asked Bill.

"I suspected earlier but became sure when Jaq made me watch the end of the interrogation recording. Jaq was right, you don't lie to God. But I was already unsure before then. Something bothered me."

"How so?" Jaq was curious.

Kiedron smiled. "You see, Erika was genuinely surprised, shocked even, when we told her that David intended to break up with her. I believed her at that moment. It could have been that David was playing some sort of a game. But I was wondering if it was something else. So, it got me thinking. I went swimming and tried to recall everything we heard about this breakup. And then I realized that we heard about David's intention to break up with Erika from only one source, and that source could have something to hide."

"Three sources," corrected Jaq. "Aubra told us first, but then Mariana Reyes and George Osborne each separately confirmed it."

"Did they?" Kiedron said with a twinkle in his eyes. "That's what we were supposed to think, but that's not quite right," he corrected her. "If you think carefully, they each heard the news second hand, from Aubra. Mariana said that Aubra told her she was happy the affair was over. Mariana never talked to David about it because they weren't friends, and she didn't even really like him. David would never discuss his affair with her. And George only found out after Aubra bought the tickets to Paris. That was after David was already dead, so he couldn't have told him. That's when I realized that this information came from only one source, which was Aubra." Kiedron took another sip of his coffee and enjoyed it in silence for a moment.

"Those tickets, that was another great misdirection," murmured Stockton almost admiringly. "Not very many people would think of that."

"Not very many people can afford to throw away the money for two first-class tickets to Europe," Jaq pointed out.

"Yes. Most people scrimp and save if they want to take an expensive vacation," agreed Kiedron. "But Aubra had money. Besides, we never found out if she bought a cancellation policy, so maybe the money wasn't completely lost. Also remember, for her, it was like buying an insurance policy of sorts. It misdirected us away from Aubra for a while, and if she got charged with murder and it came to a trial, it would play well in court."

"She had no intention of going to trial," Jaq interrupted. "She was ready with that gun. By the way, I'm still furious with myself for not checking the bathroom more carefully."

Both Kiedron and Stockton shook their heads vigorously. There was no way for Jaq to know what Aubra planned. The gun was very well hidden in the plastic box inside the toilet tank. Aubra also probably knew that she could have been arrested somewhere else. Maybe she had plans for other locations too?

"There is one more thing I'm confused about," said Bill. "Matt said that when he called David about the roses, David gave the name Flynn. Why?"

"Ah, yes," Kiedron smiled with delight. "I was wondering about this myself. And then I remembered that Erika was a movie buff, and she particularly liked the old movies. The really old movies."

"The Hollywood Golden Age movies from the 1930s and 40s! The ones with Errol Flynn as a heartthrob!" exclaimed Jaq. "Now it makes sense. That was the nickname she had for David."

"Yes. She was watching one of those movies when I first visited her," remembered Kiedron. "Good work, team!" Kiedron toasted his coworkers with the coffee. "Time to solve another murder."

Acknowledgements

This book wouldn't be possible without help from several awesome people. My early reader, Valerie Hecht, provided valuable feedback that helped me iron out some wrinkles before they became a problem. Karen Kimes helped my writing to sound more native. Thank you both for your friendship and support.

Thanks to Danny Reyna for providing the law enforcement perspective between pickleball games.

My Mom, Ewa (Krystyna) Sommerfeld-Makuta, has always been cheering me on, always ready to suggest crazy ideas to make the story move along.

Most of all, I want to thank my husband, Ken Bown, for his enthusiastic and unwavering support, no matter what.

www.ingramcontent.com/pod-product-compliance
Lightning Source LLC
Chambersburg PA
CBHW052032150726

48002CB00002B/568